Fool's

Wisdom

Jay Heavner

Canaveral Publishing

Fool's Wisdom

Jay Heavner

Cover design by Fineline Printing, Titusville, Florida

Mr. Heavner can be contacted at jay@jayheavner.com

I'd like to dedicate this book to all the men and women who served in Vietnam. All gave some. Some gave all. They were not welcomed back home with open arms and parades like veterans of past wars, which they deserved. No war is pretty. They never are. These men and women were sent to do a dirty job, and they did the best they could without the support of many in our nation or Congress. You defended what you loved, America. Thank you for your service.

And to my pastor, Malcolm Wild, from whom I first heard of Fool's Wisdom.

Acknowledgments

Many thanks to Kathleen Nadeau for opening my eyes to the history of the Cherokee people, to Ritchie at PSL for his help on guns, Doc Holladay of Sky Soldiers who took time and told me of his experiences in Vietnam during the Ia Drang Valley battle, and thanks to Sky Soldiers from American Aviation Heritage Foundation for the ride in the Huey helicopter.

Thanks to all the pastors of Calvary Chapel Merritt Island, Malcolm Wild, Howard Davies, who substitutes as the older brother I never had, Logan Dalton, Len Fedorowicz, and a *Vielen Dank* to Thomas Domajnko for his help with the German language. Thanks for all the years of excellent teaching reflected in this book.

Thanks to Mary Lou Wagoner for the encouragement and being the first reader of my book and to Tim Mace, my second reader.

To the people of the Tri-state area around Cumberland, Maryland, who have welcomed me and my books about the region with open arms.

To the ladies of my home town library at Fort Ashby WV, you'll never know how much your encouragement helped.

And to all my readers who sent me notes on how they enjoyed my books and then asked for more. Thanks for the kind words.

Any my wife, Vivian, who when I told her I thought I could write a book, said, "Well, why don't you?" Thank you for sharing the highs and lows of my writing activities and experiences.

Thanks to the late Tony Hillerman, whose mystery books set on the Navajo Nation first gave m the idea of writing a novel.

And to JoAnn and Tom Peterson for their help, JoAnn for her editing and proofing and Tom, for his help with getting the military rankings right. To Space Coast Writers, especially Dr. Valerie Allen and to a fellow writer, Mark Mynheir, for their encouragement and advice. There were many more who gave suggestions and help. Thanks to you, too.

Fool's Wisdom

Prologue

Autumn 1995

He felt like the weight of the world was on his shoulders. How he needed his mountain. If he could find peace from his many problems anywhere on this planet, it would be there. The day had a mediocre beginning and then spiraled downward steadily.

It was late afternoon on Friday when Tom Kenney made it to the old field on top of Knobley Mountain. He could look both east and west and see the state of Maryland, but where he stood was a sliver of Mineral County in West Virginia that stuck into the other state like a knife. The Potomac River was the state line, and the linear mountain forced the river to make its long horseshoe detour around it.

Tom was the owner and operator of Knobley Mountain Bottled Water, LLC. He managed the company with help from his son, Doug, but he was the one that got the call when things were stretched thin. Today, that meant working, taking a full load of water on the flatbed to a good customer, White Tails Nudist Park, near Paw Paw, WV. They had some special event this weekend and needed a truckload of bottled water. As usual, they'd waited until the last moment to place the order. Usually, he could take the service road at the resort that avoided the public area, but not today. That road was closed by construction. A new water line and the sewer line was being installed to replace old pipes that failed. Tom knew the old way to the loading dock, so he took it, but when he reached the place on the road where the hard surface was removed because of the construction project, the truck's wheels sank into the soft dirt and became stuck, very stuck, buried to the axle stuck.

Soon, Tom and the stuck truck were the centers of attention of about 40 nudists who came to see the excitement. The resort sent a forklift to unload the flatbed where it sat. It took a little less than ten minutes to unload a pallet, run it to the storage area, come back, and get the rest, all nine more. Poor Tom got his eyes full and overflowing. How he wished he had an unsee button he could push for the many unpleasant things he'd witnessed in his life. Why some of them went in the altogether like that, Tom had no idea. Some people had no shame, he figured. Flabby, naked Baby Boomers weren't a pretty sight. Only doctors wanted to see these people in the altogether, and they demanded a high fee for that.

He got the truck back to the warehouse shortly before noon in time for lunch with his

pregnant wife, Joann. They lived in the old farmhouse between the warehouse and West Virginia Highway Route 28. Joann said she was tired and wanted a nap. That was a good thing for Tom. How he desired to go to his thinking place on top of the mountain behind his house. So much had happened lately. He wished he'd never heard of Braddock's Gold. It seemed to have brought him nothing but trouble.

The question he had for God was, "Why?" He had so many whys he wanted to ask. Why had he ever listened to Johnny? Why had Chris died and not him? Why had his first wife Sarah been killed by a drunk driver? Why had God let his son Brian commit suicide? Why had God ever let him get mixed up with this Braddock's Gold matter? He'd narrowly missed death three times because of the missing French & Indian War payroll. He feared it would still get him killed. How would all this end? And now, his second wife, ten years his junior, was expecting their child, and it had been and would continue to be a precarious pregnancy. He knew how old Job in the

Bible must have felt as he wondered why? Job lost his many children and all his wealth in one day. Why? Would he have the same testimony as Job or not? Even in his dark times, Job could say, "God knows the way I take; when He has tested me, I will come forth as gold."

Lord, I know You direct my path. You say You delight in every detail of all Your children's lives. We stumble, but You keep us from falling. You hold us in Your hand. You tell us to cast all our cares on You, but sometimes they feel like a mountain on our backs.

Oh, Lord, I feel like I'm still fighting on a battlefield. I long for the day when every oppression and distress, every tear, suffering, and pain, and every wrong and injustice will be explained. Lord, today I struggle with life's unanswered questions, but I can find help and hope in Your love and promises even if I don't understand now.

Lord, let me not be a fool who despises You, but a fool for You, waiting for Your understanding and wisdom. A fool for You has more wisdom than all the wisdom ever whizzed by the so-called wise of this world.

Lord, You provide for us in surprising ways. You're not bound by my expectations. I don't know why or what You'll choose to do. I'll wait and focus on You and try to be satisfied.

Lord, help me accept Your provision and the way You choose to give it. I know You care for me and will meet my needs even though I don't understand it any better than old Job did. Amen.

A calm swept over Tom he hadn't felt in what seemed like an eternity. He piled up fallen leaves from a maple tree and lay down on them in the warm autumn sunshine. Tom pulled his Pittsburgh Steeler cap down over his face, shut his eyes, and in a few short moments, he was fast asleep and in dreamland.

Chapter 1

Tom had just nodded off. He woke with a start. The cell phone in his pocket was vibrating wildly. Half-asleep, he pulled the clamshell phone out, flipped it open, and put it to his ear.

"Hello?" he asked.

"Good afternoon, Mr. Tom Kenney," came the ever-changing, mechanical, and evil voice from the phone. "I hope I am not interrupting anything important you may be doing like taking a nap."

Tom felt like he'd been hit with a brick. The voice was that of the person who called himself The Benefactor, the nemesis who'd kidnapped him and had threatened to kill him if Tom didn't tell him where the lost payroll was. Tom's Post Traumatic Stress Disorder condition prevented him from remembering. When Tom could not satisfy The Benefactor with what he had wanted, The Benefactor had tested Tom, told Tom he would give him a lethal dose of morphine, but only knocked Tom unconscious and not killed him. As The Benefactor had told Tom later, "You are no good to me dead. Someday, your memory would return, and you **will** give me the information I want."

A voice coming from the phone startled Tom back to reality. "Hello, Mr. Kenney, are you still there?"

Tom found his voice. "Yes, I'm here. You surprised me. How did you know I was taking a nap? Are you watching me?"

The Benefactor ignored the question. "Has your memory recovered anymore? Are you any closer to remembering where the millions of dollars' worth of gold coins are located? I cannot wait forever."

"No, I'm sorry to say, nothing more has come back. I've tried to make sense of it all and come to some conclusions and answers. You told me earlier in our conversations, I'd been to the old farm off Dan's Run Road one mile from the village of Patterson Creek twice, and it concerned Braddock's Gold. Each time you said I nearly was killed. I still can't remember, but I have this bullet wound scar on my head to prove something did happen. I woke up in the VA hospital after each event. Nothing more has come back to me. All I know is what you filled-in in previous conversations. From the information, I have concluded this; somewhere on that farm is some or all of the gold or information which can lead to it, or possibly both. There's something big missing in this picture, but I still can't see it."

There was silence from the other end of the line, and after what seemed an eternity to Tom though it was only a few short seconds, Tom heard The Benefactor say, "I agree with your conclusion. I have arrived at the same. This is useful, but there is a slight problem. The authorities have also come to the same conclusion, and are watching the farm like a hawk, but give it time. They will lose interest, but only a fool would go there now."

Tom said, "I'm sorry, but I have nothing new to add to this update."

"I was afraid you would tell me something like this. Just the same, I wish to thank you for telling me about your 'friend,' Morty," said The Benefactor.

"You mean our friend, 'Mortality,' don't you?"

The Benefactor replied, "Yes, you are correct. My thinking has been rather one track lately, and I had forgotten to look at the big picture. Sometimes, one must stop and review. You might say, smell the roses on your journey."

"That is very true, but remember, even the beautiful rose has thorns."

"What are you trying to say?" asked The Benefactor.

Tom replied, "When you look at the big picture, the main thing to make certain is your main thing really the main thing? What is your main reason for living?"

"Very good question, Mr. Kenney," said The Benefactor.

Tom replied, "I believe God has used all events in my life to bring me to this point."

The Benefactor said, "You must have lived a charmed life, Mr. Kenney."

"Hardly, but my God has always been there even when I did not see it. He was guiding me through all of my troubles," said Tom.

"You are an interesting person, Mr. Kenney. You continue to give me much to think about. It would also be good if you think on remembering where Braddock's lost gold payroll is. Have a nice day, and I hope you can get back to sleep," said the Benefactor.

The phone clicked, and the line went dead.

Back to my nap? He ***is*** *watching me. Well, he's going to be bored because I am going to lie down and try to finish my rest. My God's watching too, and nothing will happen to me He does not allow. He will take care of me.*

Tom exhaled profoundly and felt some better.

Habakkuk!

Tom jumped! *Who said that?* Tom looked around, but there was no one there.

Habakkuk!!

There it was again. Tom looked in a complete circle around him but saw no one.

Habakkuk!!!

And then Tom understood. The Old Testament verse, Habakkuk 3:19, flashed in his mind. *The Lord is my strength. He makes my feet like deer's feet and enables me to go in high places.*

He remembered seeing the deer and bighorn sheep out West on the mountain ledges so thin it seemed impossible in the natural for them to be there and not fall. *Dear God, make my feet as steady as those of the deer, so I can walk in confidence at the great heights when my enemies pursue me. Let me walk in Your strength. Amen.*

It had to be a message from God. Old Habakkuk, a little known Old Testament prophet, had pointedly asked God why evil men prosper and threaten His people. God told him to watch and wait. He, God, was using the wicked men to do His work for a season. Habakkuk was to live by faith, watch and wait. His answer would come. Evil would be judged and not prevail. Habakkuk trembled at the words of the Lord. He wasn't to be afraid, and the Old Prophet jumped for joy before the Lord.

Yes, Habakkuk. I'm to be like Habakkuk. A pleasant smile came to Tom's face. *I must not be afraid.* With that, Tom lay back down on the bed of leaves and closed his eyes. His breathing became rhythmic, and he drifted off to sleep.

Chapter 2

April 1965 At the Kenney home place along WV Route 28, Short Gap, WV

Tom Kenney sat at the table in the old farmhouse he'd known as home his whole life. He was having a hard time sorting out all of the information his father had just given him. When his father told him he needed to talk, Tom's heart sank lower than whale dung in the deepest ocean. His worst fears were realized. His father knew about the events of last Saturday, and he was a dead man walking. He knew his father was going to read him the riot act. Tom was dead meat and about to be grounded for life, or longer. And worse of all, Tom had let down the man who cared for him and raised him after his mother died when Tom was small. He couldn't bear the look of disappointment he knew was coming. Still, there'd been something thrilling about what he'd been a part of. It had to feel similar to what a drug high must be like. That both frightened him and thrilled him.

His father sat down at the table and had a manila folder in his hand. He laid it in front of Tom and told him to open it. Tom was sure it was evidence of his misdeeds. Instead, the first thing he saw was a picture of his mother at about age sixteen. My, she was a beauty. He could see why his dad was attracted to her at first sight. She had long dark hair, light olive skin, and dark, almost coal-black eyes that shone like two embers in her head. And at the bottom in the margin, someone had written in ink, Goodland Cherokee Orphanage School. Surprise, he looked up from the picture. His dad said, "Tom, it's time I told you about your mother. I know you don't remember much about her. You were so young when she passed. It was hard for both of us. There never was a better woman created on this earth. Cancer took her from us way too soon."

He stopped and wiped a tear from his cheek. "I still miss her dancing eyes and that sweet smile. How she ever kept those in that hole they called a school, I'll never know. But she did, and that's what first attracted me to her. I had just got back from military service with Uncle Sam in Europe after WWII. One of the soldiers I had fought alongside of through France and Germany told me of his home in North Carolina, and he asked me if I wanted to have some R and R time in the mountains there. It sounded like a pretty good idea to me, a cot and meals and no one shooting at me. So, we went from the port in Norfolk, Virginia, by bus to the hills, I mean the mountains of western North Carolina.

"I thought we had mountains here in West Virginia, and we do have them all over the state, but those mountains there seemed like they went up to the very face of God. My buddy got us jobs working at the Indian Orphanage. He was a good talker. He could sell refrigerators to the Eskimos. He told them that we were all-around handymen, and soon we were fixin' up that old place best we could and learning how to do it as we went. It didn't take me long to see this place was no paradise. The government's policy with Indians at that time was to de-Indian the Indian out of the Indian to save the Indians. I saw some of the kids beaten if they spoke Cherokee or did anything that had anything Indian attached to it.

"It was there I met your Mom. She told me she was dropped off at the orphanage when she was just a baby. She never knew who her parents were, but from what little records she found, she was either full blood Cherokee or at least half. To make a long story short, we fell in love. She was sixteen at the time. With the money I saved up, I bought an old rattletrap car, and we used it to make our escape from the orphanage. No one ever looked for her. They were happy to be rid of another mouth to feed. She'd have to leave anyway as soon as she came of age. With her looks, she could pass for a white person, and that's what we did when we got home here. Your grandpa, I think, suspected something was up, but he never did say anything. We lived in this old house with my maw and paw for many years. When they got old and feeble, she was the one who took care of them. She was a good woman. You came along in 1947, and she now had three besides herself to care for. I don't know how she did it, but she did. She was a fine woman, like one of those virtuous women they talk about in the Bible.

"So what I wanted to tell you was, Tom, you are either half Cherokee or at least a quarter. Back then, there was kind of a bad stigma in being mixed race, and I know there still is some, but this is something I thought you were ready for. You're like your mom. Very little of the Indian shows."

Tom was stunned and said so. He looked at the other pictures in the folder. Each one had his mother in it. Some were with his dad. Some had her with his grandparents. A few were group pictures, and a few were of him with his mother. Tom wanted to tear up when he saw these, but he fought it. The youth didn't want anyone to think he wasn't manly. Sissies cried. His father saw this turmoil in Tom but said nothing. He knew what was going on in the young man.

Finally, his dad said, "I'll leave you here with these for now so you can look at them. I got to get off to work."

He rose from the table and headed for the door. He grabbed his coat and hat off the clothes pole by the back door. Tom noticed a little tremor in his dad's right hand. Then, he turned to Tom, and dryly said, "Try to stay out of trouble today." And with that, he was gone.

Tom's stomach churned a little. The story must have really shaken up his dad. His dad's hands had always been so steady and firm. And it seemed his dad knew more than he was saying, or did he? Tom looked at the pictures for another ten minutes or so and then heard the wheels of the black '57 Chevy on the dirt and gravel coming up to the house. It stopped around the back, and the driver honked the horn. Tom took one last look at the first picture he'd seen in the folder, the photo of his mother. He sighed and closed the folder. Tom grabbed his coat and ball hat off of the clothes pole and headed out the back door.

"Hey buddy, you look like you seen a ghost. You okay?" questioned the driver.

"Yeah, I'll be all right. I just heard some surprising news. It'll all work out somehow. You still want to go through with this?"

"Damn straight. I wouldn't miss this for the world," the driver replied.

"Then, let's do it. I love it when a plan comes together."

The driver smiled a satisfied grin. "Then, what's keeping us? Let's get with it."

The driver backed up the hotrod, put it in Drive, went down the gravel and dirt driveway, stopped at WV Route 28, waited for a truck heading for Fort Ashby to go by, then turned left toward Cumberland, Maryland, and their day with destiny.

Chapter 3

Saturday, one week earlier.

Tom would be graduating from high school soon, but he was unsure of his plans after that. He'd probably get a job at one of the local factories. The dark-haired beauty he'd been dating was going off to college, and he figured he'd not be seeing much of her once that happened. She'd get her college degree, a B.S. of some sort, and also her Mrs. as so many of the girls he knew would and did.

His life had been a lot more exciting since he had met Johnny Johnson. He'd shown up for classes at Fort Ashby High School at the beginning of the school year. No one seemed to know where he came from. Students were usually seated alphabetically in their classes, and Tom Kenney found himself next to Johnny Johnson. They'd made small talk at first, but over time had become close classmates and friends. One day, Johnny mentioned he had gotten into some minor trouble in North Carolina, and his parents believed it best if he had a change of location for a while. He now lived with his aunt and uncle, who was the mayor of the neighboring town of Ridgeley. Tom wondered why Johnny didn't go to school at Ridgeley High, but he never asked. All he knew was Johnny always had money for fun and was looking for someone, a co-conspirator, as he laughingly referred to the position Tom had taken as his sidekick. Johnny told him to be ready about 7:00 AM. They'd go over to Cumberland for some fun. Tom was not sure what this fun was, but he knew with Johnny at the helm, there would be excitement.

Johnny showed up at seven in his black, souped-up '57 Chevy. He had those distinctive tailpipes on his car that made the exhaust rumble, so you'd hear him coming before he actually got there if you had youthful ears, which his dad didn't. He was rarely late. Tom slipped out of the back door of the old farmhouse. He had left a short note for his dad telling him that he had gone to town with his friend and would be back by lunchtime. His dad had not been feeling well lately and seemed to be sleeping more than he usually did.

Tom opened the passenger's door to the hot rod and slid into the seat. "You ready for some fun?" asked Johnny.

"Yeah, answered Tom. "Let the good times roll."

The two young men made small talk as they roared toward Cumberland. They talked about school, girls, cars, what to do after graduation that, and other things that fill a 17-year-old male's mind. There was a lot of talk about girls, especially the ones they'd heard were easy.

They crossed the bridge over the Potomac River and proceeded to the South End Donut and Bagel Shop in the commercial area on Industrial Boulevard. Johnny pulled the car into the parking lot, but away from the store near the busy street.

"So this is the big fun surprise you had?" snickered Tom. "Coffee and donuts. You've made the big leagues."

"You just wait. You remember those two booger eatin' useless flatfoot cops I was telling you about that harassed me anytime they found me over here across the river?"

Tom nodded. "What have you got in mind?"

"Today, I'm getting even. Did you see those big rubber bumper guards I put on the back?"

"Yeah, I saw them. I wondered what they were for."

"Revenge, sweet revenge." Tom saw a black and white Cumberland Police Car pulling into the parking lot.

"Duck! It's them!" The patrol car pulled up to the front door directly behind the black Chevy. The two cops exited the vehicle and reappeared shortly, each carrying a monster cup of steaming coffee and three donuts. "Those guys are so predictable," chuckled Johnny. Now the fun begins."

Tom smiled at Johnny. *This should be good.* Johnny started the car. He watched as the cops opened their coffee cups and began to take bites out of the donuts.

"It don't git no better than this," Johnny said with a satisfying grin that ran from ear to ear. Slowly, he backed his Chevy up until it was almost touching the cop car. He let his foot off the brake, and it nudged the other car slightly. The cops were startled and spilled some of their coffee on themselves. Johnny put the car in drive and put about two feet of space between the two vehicles. At that point, he threw the car into reverse and gave the engine some gas. ***BAM!!!*** The two cars hit together, and coffee and donuts went flying everywhere in the patrol car. Loud curses could be heard coming from the car, and then the shout, "It's him!!"

"That's our clue to leave," Johnny said with some sarcasm.

Tom pleaded, "what are we goin' to do now?'

"Trust me. I have a plan."

"It better be a good one. Those cops are madder than wet hornets."

Before the cops had time to recover and begin their pursuit in earnest, Johnny weaved quickly through the many side streets and alleys in South Cumberland. "They'll never find us," he chuckled. And then he looked at Tom. "See, I told you we'd have some fun."

Wide-eyed, Tom looked back and blurted out, "You're crazy! You're certifiable!"

"Yeah, I know, but you got to admit it was sure fun."

A big smile came to Tom's face. "It sure was."

Johnny continued to drive around the bowels of Cumberland's back streets. He parked the car under a tree that overhung a lightly traveled side street.

"Where did you learn to drive like that?" Tom asked.

"I might as well tell you. I trust you can keep a secret. My family in the North Carolina hills makes moonshine. We run it to the bars in Charlotte and Atlanta. And the cops don't like that, so sometimes you need a hot car and driving skills to outrun, outmaneuver, and outthink them. I'd been running a lot of loads for my paw, and the cops were breathing down my neck, so he thought it would be a good idea if I left town for a while. His brother is my Uncle Bob, also known as the Mayor of Ridgeley. Capisce?"

"Wow, you sure are full of surprises. I think I have had enough for today. Let's go home."

Johnny replied, "Sounds good to me." He started the car and was soon heading in the direction of Wiley Ford, West Virginia. They went down Virginia Avenue and passed a patrol car parked in a side lot.

A curse rolled from Johnny's lips. "It's them, and they've seen us!"

The patrol car carrying two, mad, coffee-soaked cops pulled onto the streets after them. "What are you gonna do?" Tom said.

"Head for the state line. It's only a half-mile away, and they won't pursue us then."

Johnny sped up, but the cops did too, and now the boys in blue had their lights and siren on. They crossed the bridge over the Potomac that makes the state line, but the two, mad, wet cops kept coming. Tom had been watching the cop car. He turned to Johnny, "What are you gonna do now?!?"

"I got a plan." The car roared down the road with the cops right behind. They took the banked turn in front of Snyder's Grocery and headed for Ridgeley on Alternate Route 28. The two cars roared over a hill, down the other side, through several turns, and headed north on the snaking but relatively straight but narrow road. Ridgeley was two miles ahead.

Johnny picked up the hand-held microphone to the CB radio that hung from under the center dashboard. "Breaker 271, this is Cisco Kid. Do you read me?"

"We read you loud and clear. What's your 20?"

"Coming into town on the mountain road with two bandits hot on my tail. Requesting assistance. Over."

"Roger that. We'll be expecting you soon at the high school. Over."

"Roger that. ETA in two minutes and coming in very hot."

"We'll be there to welcome you."

Tom looked at Johnny and said, "We are so dead. Man. We are so dead."

"Trust me," Johnny said. "It'll all work out."

The two cars continued to roar down the narrow road. Neither slowed down when they hit the 25 mph zone at the town limits. They sped through the sleepy little town to the high school where Johnny turned a quick right through the six-foot fence that surrounded the campus. He slid to a halt with the cops right behind them.

The cops jumped out of their car with guns drawn. "On the ground! Hands on your backs," they shouted.

The two boys did as they were told. Johnny had a smirk on his face, but Tom was so scared he thought he'd wet himself. The Cumberland cops handcuffed the two and set them on the ground. They had satisfied looks on their faces. At that time, two Ridgeley Police cars appeared. The first pulled into the lot, and the second blocked the gate to the street.

The two Ridgeley cops got out of their cars and walked up to the Cumberland cops. The first Ridgeley cop said with a little sarcasm, "You boys are a little out of your jurisdiction, ain't you?"

"We were in hot pursuit," came the curt reply.

"So I heard. Your bosses are sure gonna wanna hear about this. Hot pursuit across state lines, not notifying anyone of that, and recklessly endangering only God knows how many lives with your actions. I think it would be in your best interest if you just turn this all over to us so we, who are the proper authorities, can handle it. You just move along. We'll handle this proper-like here, and try to forget you-alls was ever here."

Tom looked at Johnny, who was trying not to grin with little success. *Maybe this was going to work out.* The cops had a heated argument for several minutes, but the Ridgeley cops weren't budging. And they had the Cumberland cops boxed in. Finally, the cops from across the river realized they were in a no-win situation. They walked over to the boys and removed the handcuffs. They then got into their patrol car and drove to the entrance. One Ridgeley cop slowly sauntered to his vehicle blocking the gate. He got in, started it, and moved it out of the way. The Cumberland patrol car drove out onto the street. The one in the passenger seat looked back and saw Johnny waving goodbye to them. Even at this distance, Tom could see an angry scowl on his face. The police car disappeared down the city street toward Cumberland.

One of the two remaining cops came over to the two boys. He addressed Johnny. "You sure stepped in it this time."

"Ah, Uncle Joe, we was just havin' some fun."

"Fun? You could have got yourselves killed or worst. Fun? We haven't been on good terms with the Cumberland cops, and this ain't gonna help one bit. I hope we can keep a lid on this, and it doesn't blow up in our faces. Get outta here before I do something rash!"

Johnny said nothing more. He motioned for Tom to get in the car, which he did. Johnny started the car and drove out onto the street. Tom saw the two cops putting their heads together, and he could tell that they were working on a cover story for this whole episode. They drove up the mountain road toward Wiley Ford in silence that continued all the way to Tom's house. They pulled into the driveway. Tom got out of the car and looked back at Johnny. Before Tom could say anything, Johnny started, "I told you it was gonna be fun."

There was a pregnant pause, and then Johnny asked, "You still gonna be my friend?"

"I'll think about it," he replied. Tom turned his back on Johnny and started toward the house. He took two steps and then turned around.

"You're one wild and crazy guy," Tom said straight-faced. Then he smiled, "Let the good times roll, ole buddy. Let the good times roll. See you at school on Monday."

"All right!" Johnny exclaimed. "Let the good times roll." With that, he put the souped-up Chevy in reverse and backed up in the driveway. He shifted to drive and disappeared down the driveway to Route 28.

Tom thought, *Nothing mild and tame about that guy. He could get me in all kinds of trouble if we're not careful. I hope my dad never finds out.* But like so many young men that age, he was already addicted to the rush the excitement gave him, and he knew it. It would take an extra-large dose of reality to bring him back down to Planet Earth.

Chapter 4

Johnny showed up in his hot rod '57 Chevy the following Saturday at the old farmhouse Tom called home. It was early, and Tom knew Johnny had something big planned, but he wasn't sure what. Johnny had been dropping hints about it all week at school. "Fun," he said. "It'll be a time to remember."

Tom was interested, but just a little scared too after the car chase with the Cumberland cops last week. His dad had not said anything about it directly in his talk with Tom, so he felt maybe he'd dodged the bullet. Tom closed the door to the house, walked out to Johnny's car, and got in. "So, you got something big up your sleeve for today?"

"Damn straight. After today, those flatfoots will leave us alone."

"I got a bad feeling about this, but let's go."

The teenage adrenaline was definitely flowing freely in the two young men.

"All right! You won't forget this day!"

How right he was. With that, the young men were off. They passed down the twisting, turning road needing straightening and improvement for decades known as WV Route 28. Traffic was light. It seemed the area population was slow in rising on that weekend morn. The boys soon crossed the bridge at Wiley Ford and proceeded through the part of town known as South Cumberland. Johnny took a right off of Virginia Avenue onto Industrial

Boulevard. It was not long before he pulled into the parking lot of the donut shop where they had begun their adventure, or maybe a better word would be escapade or fiasco with the Cumberland Police a week ago. He parked the car in a distant out-of-the-way part of the lot. Tom looked at Johnny with apprehension. "Just what have you got in mind?" he asked.

"I'm gonna teach those coppers a lesson they will never forget. I've been planning this all week. I'm gonna get them to chase us down the boulevard to Mexico Farms. There's a dirt road that turns off, and near the river, it forks just over a small hill. The right fork goes to a fishin' hole, and the left fork goes to a plowed field. It ain't nothin' but muddy soup after that last rain we had. They'll be chasing us, and we take the right fork and stop right there. The cops will have to take the left fork to avoid hitting us. The hill will keep them from seeing the trap. When they go flying left, they'll get buried axle-deep in that muddy field. It will work like a charm. What could go wrong?"

Tom did not immediately answer, and there was a pregnant pause in the car. "You are still in, aren't you?" asked Johnny. "You can get out now if you want to, but you'll miss all the fun. Yah, what could go wrong?"

Tom shook his head. "Yeah, I'm in. I must be crazy, but like you said, 'what could go wrong?'"

"All right! Let the good times roll!"

The two boys kept a keen eye on the four-lane highway in front of the donut shop. About ten minutes later, a Cumberland Police car pulled into the parking lot. There were two cops in it, the same two who had chased the boys last Saturday. "Right on time and just as planned," Johnny said with a satisfied grin on his face.

The cops parked their car in the handicapped spot in front of the store and went in. Johnny started the Chevy and moved it to a place in another row directly behind the police car. The boys slid down in their seats. Several minutes later, the cops emerged, each with a fist full of donuts and a large coffee. With their hands full, they had some difficulty opening the doors and getting into the car without dropping or spilling their treasures. The two boys watched as the cops chowed down on the goodies. Johnny looked over at Tom. "Time for some fun." Tom grinned at Johnny, who smiled back.

Johnny eased the four-on-the-floor into reverse. The Chevy slowly backed across the parking lot. The big bumper guards on the boys' car gently made contact with the back of the cop car. It was enough to spill some of the coffee that the cops were sipping and get their attention. "Hey!" came a cry from the police car.

Johnny chuckled and looked at Tom. "Now, the fun begins." He put the car in first and drifted away about three feet. Quickly he threw the four-on-the-floor into reverse. "Let the good times roll!" he said with enthusiasm and slammed the Chevy into the back of the police car. Donuts and coffee went flying, and loud cursing came from the vehicle.

Johnny looked at Tom. "Told you this would be fun."

"You're crazy!" exclaimed Tom. "Get us out of here!"

"You got it!" Johnny threw the Chevy back into first gear and burned rubber getting out of the parking lot and onto the four-lane Industrial Boulevard. It didn't take long for the drenched and mad cops to be in hot pursuit.

Johnny looked into his rearview mirror and chuckled again. "Just as planned. I got them in the palm of my hand."

Tom looked at the cops. Their lights and siren were going wild. "I must have been nuts to let you talk me into this. This is insane! I'm really gonna regret this! I must be crazy!"

"Relax. What could go wrong? You'll remember this great day for the rest of your life."

"I just got a bad feeling about this. It's not gonna end well."

The two speeding cars continued down the four-lane highway. There was about 500 feet between them. The road narrowed to two lanes shortly after it crossed Evitts Creek near where the drive-in sat off to the left. Johnny roared down the curvy highway. Tom could tell he was letting the cops catch up. They neared the intersection with the Mexico Farms Road. Johnny swerved the car to the right down the dead-end road. "Bet those flatfoots think they got us now," said Johnny. Tom didn't reply. He was hoping it all worked out. *It better go as planned,* he thought.

The two cars continued down the narrow road that got narrower as they went on. "Almost there," said a smiling Johnny. Soon the fork-in-the-road would be there. They would go right and skid to a stop, and the cops would have to go left to avoid them. The soupy, muddy field would get them. Then, the two boys would laugh at the madder-than-wet-hornets cops, turn, and drive off to safety. He went around another blind curve, and the fork was right in front of him. A curse word slipped from Johnny's lips. Parked in the right fork was a green and yellow John Deere tractor, and it completely blocked the way. Johnny grabbed at the steering wheel and tore it left. His hot rod and its two passengers went through the left fork and into the muddy field. With a mighty splash of mud and muck, it skidded to a halt and sank to the axle. The two boys sat stunned in the mud-covered car. The police car slowly pulled to a stop and blocked the way out, not that the boy's car was coming out without the help of a tow truck.

The two cops got out of their car. The short policeman, who had been driving, looked at the other Cumberland cop. "Thought they might try this. They should've picked another road. I know this one. I live on it."

The second cop began to laugh, and he laughed hard. The short one walked over to where the muddy field began. "Boys," he said, "looks like you two are in a bit of a jam. Now, we can do this the easy way or the hard way. You guys are in enough trouble. Why make more?"

The two boys got out of the stuck car and sank in the mud well over their ankles. Johnny looked at Tom. "I think we better take the easy way." Tom nodded, and the two boys struggled to walk in the mud to the police. They were quickly handcuffed and placed in the back of the cop car. Neither spoke on the way back to town. They were taken to the Allegany County Jail, booked, given a jail uniform, and placed in a jail cell together. They would appear before a judge tomorrow.

Finally, Johnny spoke. "Told you this was gonna be fun. It would be something you would remember for the rest of your life."

"Remember and regret. How are we gonna get out of this? We're in up to our eyeballs."

"Trust me. I got a plan."

"Didn't you tell me that earlier today and look where your plan got us?"

"Trust me. It ain't over till the fat lady sings."

"I hope you got something big up your sleeve 'cause we could use a small miracle 'bout now."

"Trust me. I make a phone call, and I think I have one coming."

"Hope that one includes me."

"It will. I'll do my best for you, too. Don't know about you, but all this fun can wear a guy out. I'm getting some sleep. You should try to get some also. Tomorrow is gonna be a busy day. I have a sneaking feeling."

"Don't know if I can sleep after all this."

"Well, I can. Good night. You just got to make the best of it. Sleep tight." Johnny laid back and pulled the cover that looked like it came from WWII surplus over him. Soon, he was quiet and then began to snore lightly.

Tom looked at Johnny sleeping soundly. *How could he sleep after all they'd been through? What would tomorrow bring? Why had he let Johnny talk him into this?* Tom lay down on the hard bed and stared at the ceiling. He had better try to get some sleep. Johnny was right. Tomorrow was going to be a busy day. What would it bring? He closed his eyes and, like Johnny, was soon asleep, but his sleep was full of tossing and turning. There were no sweet dreams for him.

***

The Next Morning

Tom opened his sleepy eyes. He still felt tired. *Where am I?* The iron bars and concrete block walls brought him back to reality. He was in jail, awaiting a judge and a hearing. He looked around, but

Johnny was nowhere to be seen. Tom was alone in the cell, and his heart sank. He'd been abandoned. Why did he ever listen to Johnny?

A half-hour passed, but it seemed much longer. Tom heard a heavy door open and then close. Footsteps approached. A man in a guard uniform appeared. "Tom Kenney?" he asked, though it was more of a statement than a question.

"Yes."

He unlocked the door. "Come with me."

Tom did as told. The large guard directed him down a long hallway. They turned left at an intersection and went down a still longer hallway painted a drab gray. "In here," the guard directed.

Tom went into the well-lit room and saw his father sitting in a chair at a small bolted-down table. The guard directed him to sit across from his dad, left the room, and locked the door behind him. Tom looked at his dad. A tear rolled from Tom's eye. "Dad, I messed up big time. I'm sorry."

His dad looked at him. "Yeah, you did." They sat in silence for a long moment.

"Dad, I …" But his dad cut him off.

"Yeah, you messed up big time." He held his thoughts and began again. "It may feel like the end of the world, but we'll get through this. Are you wondering where your friend is?"

"Yeah, it looks like he threw me under the bus and took off."

"He's gone, but let me tell you the whole story. You ever wonder what he was doing up here?" Tom nodded his head. "His family has, shall we say, connections. He needed that fast car because they run bootleg moonshine out of the hills of North

Carolina to Charlotte, Atlanta, and other places. Your friend's family pulled some strings and greased some palms. Johnny is on his way home to North Carolina on the condition he never returns to this area."

"So he left me up-the-creek-without-a-paddle?"

"Well, he didn't forget you. I don't have any money to spread around to buy off the law here. The best deal his family's lawyer could get was this. You get a get-out-of-jail-free card if you agree to certain conditions."

"What are they?"

"You come home with me so you can graduate, and you stay out of Cumberland till this dies down."

"That sounds much better than I could ever have imagined."

"There's more. After graduation, you're going to the military. The judge and me think the Army would be the right place for you."

Tom's shoulders shrugged. "The military! That sure wasn't what I'd planned."

"You get an honorable discharge, and the whole thing will be expunged from your record. You're still seventeen. They can do that. If you don't complete this, they could come back and throw the book at you."

"The military? It's got to beat doin' time in jail. It sure wouldn't be my first choice, but I guess the alternative is a lot worse. Okay."

"Good. We can get through this. Jailer? We're ready."

They could hear the key turning in the lock. The door opened, and the guard stood in the exit way. "So, he took it, did he? I think you made a wise decision, young man. Make it work. I don't ever want to see you in here again, understood?"

"Yes sir," said Tom.

"Yes sir," repeated the guard. "I think he might make it. He's off to the right start. I'll take you to the judge."

It all went as they had said. The judge read Tom the riot act and then set him free with a stern warning. "If you don't complete this agreement, the State of Maryland will see you're punished to the full extent the law allows."

Tom said he understood. The judge slammed the gavel down hard and told them to leave, which they did as quickly as possible. The men exited the courthouse. It was bright out. Tom put his hand up to shade his eyes from the sun. It had never looked so good. They rode to the old farmhouse they called home in silence.

A week later, Tom graduated from Fort Ashby High School in the class of 1965, 55 boys and girls. Tom walked down the aisle with a dark-haired gal named Betty Jean. She was headed off to college at Shepherd State. And Tom was headed off to boot camp. He wondered if he would ever see her again or anyone in his hometown. It seemed like he was walking to the end of the world and jumping off. This wasn't at all what he could have dreamed in his worst nightmare.

Chapter 5

Tom sat on the porch he'd known as home. How different it felt now, and he'd only been away a few months. The morning air was already warm. It was going to be a hot one this early August day. The long Beatle-like hair he had disappeared on the first day of boot camp. The barbers at Camp Jackson had made sure every man looked the same. The last time Tom had that little hair on his head was at birth. His dad, a veteran of WWII, had given him a warning about boot camp. "You just gotta get through it," he said. "Boot camp is like a prisoner of war camp with a few differences. They're restricted from hitting you. They can't kill you, but they can make you wish you were dead. You just gotta get through it."

That's what Tom had done. It was, "Yes, drill sergeant. No, drill sergeant." He'd said little more to the man who had pushed him further and harder than he'd ever been pushed in his young life. There were countless marches back and forth, forth and back, up hills, down hills, around hills, and through rivers and smelly swamps. He slept in leaky tents and on the hard ground, ate rations manufactured for WWII that made him long for anything else and got cussed at a lot like all the other grunts. He knew he didn't want to be the one who stood out like Gomer Pyle. Those that did got special attention for the drill sergeant. Boot camp was bad enough without that.

He had two weeks leave before he was to report to Camp Benning in Georgia for his next phase of army life. It was something new some high-level brass has dreamed up, air infantry. Under this new idea, the foot soldier not only could walk to battle but be transported in by helicopter. He'd been picked for this because he'd made Marksman in shooting. All that hunting for squirrels, rabbits, deer, and other small animals had made him a crack shot, and that's what the Army wanted. His path in the Army had been determined for him.

It was a long ride home from South Carolina. The old Greyhound bus took the interstate highways where they'd been completed, but Tom saw more two-lane roads than he cared for. About the only good thing that had come from the long trip was that he had met another GI on the bus. The shaved head gave it away. He had initially been seated behind Tom. Early in the long ride, Tom had turned and spoken to him. His name was Hairston, Bill Hairston, and he was from Keyser, West Virginia. When the man next to him got off the bus at a stop in Fort Dobbs, North Carolina, Tom had moved back and taken the seat next to Bill. They chatted about their homes back in the hills of West Virginia. Bill had just graduated from Keyser High School and been a guard on their basketball team. He reminded Tom how the Golden Tornados had put a whuppin' on the Eagles of Fort Ashby High. To Bill's chagrin, Tom told him he forgave him for the whuppin'. After that, the two got along just fine, and both of them being Steeler fans didn't hurt either. Bill had just finished boot camp, also at Camp Jackson, though their paths hadn't crossed there. He, too, had left and was to report to Camp Benning for the new air infantry. Bill said he came from a poor family, and the military was his ticket out. Even though he had never fired a gun before, he also made Marksman at boot camp and had been picked to go to this new unit. And Bill was black. Tom had never been around many black people before. In Tom's small world, there had just not been any black people. He told this to Bill. Bill responded, "Black folks are pretty much like white folk, just tryin' to make a livin' and keep the wolf away from the door. Don't matter what color of skin a man has on the outside, we all bleed red." Tom could see the wisdom in that logic.

The front door to the old farmhouse opened, and Tom's dad walked out. Something seemed different about him. He seemed slower, and Tom thought he saw his father's left hand tremble slightly. He sat down in the old chair next to his son. "So, how was boot camp?"

"About like you said, Dad. And maybe even a little worse than you described."

"Yeah, I thought so. They don't want to make it too easy on you. They have to weed out the weak that would be a drag on the unit. I'm proud of you, son. You made it through and made Marksman too. Guess all that killing of pop bottles and tin cans we did with the .22 when you were growing up paid off."

Tom said he was glad for all the practice time spent with his Dad and then told him about the GI from Keyser he'd met on the bus.

"Some people are just gifted like that," his dad said. "They never know they have it in them until they try it."

There was a moment's silence between them — the cars zipped by on WV Route 28. Tom had never really noticed the traffic on the nearby highway before. He had just grown up with it until it was part of the scenery.

"You'll do good at this new camp. Do what they tell you. Learn all you can. It will help keep you alive. I don't want to lose my only son," his dad said.

"Hey, I'm not planning on getting myself killed. I…," but his father cut him off.

"Listen to me, son. No one plans on getting themself killed, but it happens. I seen many a man die when I fought in Europe. Dying ain't pretty, and it can happen to any soldier."

The two men sat in silence again, and then Tom's dad spoke. "Seems to me this war in Vietnam is heating up. I don't like what I see. After WWII and Korea, I don't know if the nation is ready for another war. And this guy in the White House, Johnson, I don't trust him. He says all the right things, but it seems to me he'd leave you twisting in the wind if it was a political advantage for him."

Tom had never heard his dad speak like this, and it surprised him.

A long moment passed before the elder Kenney spoke, "I want you to be careful and come back home in one piece. I love you, son, and don't know what I'd do if something happened to you."

Tom didn't know what to say. He reached over and took his dad's hand that trembled slightly. "I love you too, Dad, and will work at makin' sure I come back home okay." He noticed that his dad's hand continued to shake. "Why is your hand shakin', Dad?"

His dad looked away and spoke, "Oh, it's nothin'. I'm just kinda shook up thinkin' about you goin' off in this big ole hostile world. Be careful. I don't wanna see nothin' bad happen to you."

Tom looked at his dad. How he loved the man who had raised him, the man who'd been both father and mother to him after his mom was taken by cancer. He gave the old man a big hug. "I love you, Dad, and I'll do my best to make it home in one piece." His dad nodded his head in agreement. "Hey, Dad, I heard there was a new restaurant, Linda's, just opened up about a mile from here toward Cumberland. How about I spend some of that newly found GI wealth and take you there?"

"Okay, best offer I've had all day. This will be a treat - you payin' for something for me out of your own pocket. Do you remember when you were little and asked for money to buy me a Christmas gift?"

"Yeah, Dad, I do. My treat today. Your little boy's growin' up. The world's there for me to conquer."

"Be careful, my son. I don't think you have any idea what's in store for you."

Chapter 6

Tom got ready to ship out. He was part of an elite experimental combat division trained in the new art of airmobile warfare ordered by President John Kennedy, now dead for two years. The division received the colors of the historic 1st Cavalry Division, and all proudly sewn on the big yellow and black shoulder patches with the horse head silhouette. His country and the new president asked him to go to war, and he felt it was his duty to go.

Tom remembered the departing words of his commander, "Men, we are going to war. You will be on the battlefield. There you will discover that in that depressing, hellish place where death is your constant companion, that we love one another. We kill for each other. We die for each other. And we weep for each other. We will come to love each man there with us as a brother. In battle, your world will shrink to the man on your right or the man on your left as the enemy is all around. You will hold each other's lives in your hands. You will share each other's fears and hopes and dreams as readily as you share what little good luck that comes your way.

"This is not a movie. When it's over, the dead do not get up, dust themselves off, and walk away. The wounded do not wash off the red and go on with life unhurt. Even those who somehow will escape miraculously unscratched will by no means be untouched. No one will be the same when you leave as when you arrive. May God go with you and watch over you while you are in Vietnam." And as an afterthought, he added these words of Shakespeare, "We few, we happy few, we band of brothers; for he today who sheds his blood with me shall be my brother." It was only much later after he returned to America, would he fully understand the commander's words.

In mid-August, the battalion was loaded onto buses, transported to Charleston, South Carolina, and then boarded the *USNS Maurice Rose*. It took most of a month for the ship to travel to Vietnam by way of the Panama Canal. They established a base at Khe, 42 miles west of Qui Nhon. The Army couldn't have picked a worse spot. It was like an old West fort smack dab in the middle of Indian country. With the help of two thousand local laborers armed with axes and machetes, they hacked a base from the dense forest. At night, the enemy probed the base for weaknesses with little success. The malaria-carrying mosquitoes caused far more casualties to the battalion.

Word came down from the top. General Dick Knowles issued an order to all men, "Find the enemy and go after them." Information on the enemy's location was lacking. By chance, the order reached the ears of a sniper from Maryland named Wayne Mullenax. He'd been out in the jungle for days bagging as he called his job. Daily, he'd take out three or four of the enemy with his specially equipped M14. Mullenax accidentally stumbled onto someone from back home, Tom Kenney, who'd asked if he'd seen the enemy during their conversation. Mullenax said that if you wanted to find the enemy, they were thicker than fleas on a stray dog, to the west, in the area of the Ia Drang valley.

Ia meant river in the local Montagnard people's dialect. The information on the enemy was passed on to the higher-ups. Recons went out. Evidence of the enemy was found, and landing sites for the air infantry were selected. Among them was X-Ray, an irregular clearing about the size of a football field in the dense jungle. On November 14, Tom Kenney, Chris Benally, and Bill Hairston were among the first of a dozen men sent in with orders to secure the landing site over 14 miles in hostile territory and to hold it. There were no roads for a retreat. Food was C-rations only, cans of ham and lima beans, spaghetti with meatballs, or beans and franks that they could zip open with P-38 can openers everyone wore on their dog-tags around their necks along with guns, grenades, and all the ammo they could carry and more. Everything seemed to be going fine as the choppers brought about 80 men off. A perimeter was set up with guards for the night. The rest of the men were told to get some sleep. It might be a long time before they got another chance. They pulled ponchos from their packs. The men rolled up in them on the ground and went to sleep with weapons close at hand.

The next morning, evidence of enemy activity was seen around the clearing. They called in artillery to pound the nearby jungle. If all went well, the choppers would be there shortly afterward to further soften up any remaining enemy with rockets, grenades, and machine gunfire. If the timing or coordinates were off, the landing choppers and men on the ground would not live to see the morning through. Today, it went well, and more men and supplies arrived in the Hueys, which came in hot. Even Tom, a greenhorn in battle, could tell something felt wrong. There was nothing wrong, except that nothing was wrong and that was unmistakably not right. It was too smooth and easy. By noon, the area filled with members of Alpha and Bravo companies. Patrols went out, and one brought back a prisoner, a scrawny, wild-eyed young man who trembled with fear. He was unarmed and barefoot, wore dirty, torn khaki trousers, and had an empty canteen, no papers, no food, and no ammunition.

Tom watched as the short interrogation of the frightened young man was carried out. He didn't like the look of apprehension he saw on the translator's face. "What did he say? Where are they?" a young lieutenant asked.

"He says there are three battalions on the mountain who want very much to kill many Americans, but haven't because they have been unable to find any."

Tom's stomach churned as he realized what was wrong. They had landed in the eye of a hurricane, and it would soon be moving. If the enemy could gain control of the landing site, their supply line, their lifeline would be gone, and all would die here. Tom heard shots ring out in the nearby brush. The battle for Landing Zone X-Ray had begun.

Chapter 7

When first under fire an' you're wishful to duck,
Don't look nor take 'eed at the man that is struck,
Be thankful you're livin', and trust to your luck
And march to your front like a soldier.

Rudyard Kipling, "The Young British Soldier"

The battle had barely begun, but chaos was already breaking out. Units fractionalized, the antagonists searched blindly for each other, chaos reigned, but somehow, a battle formed from the mess. One gung-ho lieutenant led his unit into the brush, chasing after the enemy. They disappeared out of sight and became separated from the main body at X-Ray. Two-hundred-and-fifty men remained at the land zone. Bullets whizzed by, shot from small arms and automatic weapons. Sporadic mortar and rocket fire came in. Men lying on the ground screamed in pain when hit, but they'd survived the bullets. Those that didn't scream hadn't. The medics worked frantically as the bodies began to pile up.

Tom found a fallen tree, crawled behind it, and fired at anything that moved outside of the perimeter in the brush. Two men fell in next to him. He turned and looked into the faces of the commanding officer of the ground operation and his radioman. The latter's face was a pale white. "Soldier," the commander yelled. "Keep the lead firing. We need cover so I can call in airstrikes. We may have the same designation as Custer, but we've got something he didn't have, fire support. We ain't goin' down like he did at Little Bighorn."

"Yes, sir," Tom said, and he lay down as much deadly covering fire with his M16 as possible. Above the din, Tom heard the commander screaming at someone named Dillon for airstrikes, artillery, and rockets. The enemy mortars were killing them, he yelled. Air support must find and eliminate them.

Within minutes, the air filled with red dust and smoke as the deluge of destruction rained hell from the sky. Tom thought it was awesome, and its thunder was music to his ears. Artillery rounds hissed above him along with the easily recognized sound of incoming, followed by the detonations close by. Helicopters swooped in from above, and a whooshing sound meant they had unleashed their deadly 2.75-inch rockets. Shattering blasts were heard from all directions as fighter-bombers dropped 250 and 500-pound bombs and napalm canisters. Rifles, machine guns, mortars, and exploding grenades added to the deafening noise and chaos.

Tom looked around, but the two other men were nowhere to be seen. Where they'd gone, he did not know. He saw another man crawling toward him. It was Bill, and he yelled to him, "Bill, over here." He yelled again, and this time Bill heard him. He turned to crawl toward him. Just as he got to Tom's position, a bullet ripped through Bill's neck. His face filled with pain. He rose up and was hit again. At this time, a grenade rolled in next to him, and Bill fell on it. A quick second later, it exploded, killing the already mortally wounded Bill. The concussion from the explosion blew Tom backward. He laid still, stunned and unconscious.

Chapter 8

The guns o' the enemy wheel into line,
Shoot low at the limbers an' don't mind the shine,
For noise never startles the soldier.
Start, start, startles the soldier…

If your officer's dead and the sergeants look white,
Remember it's ruin to run from a fight:
So take open order, lie down, and sit tight,
And wait for supports like a soldier.
Wait, wait, wait like a soldier…

Rudyard Kipling, The Young British Soldier

Tom woke up to the whoop-whoop-whoop sound of choppers nearby. He looked to the side and saw the mangled body of his friend, Bill. He'd saved Tom's life by falling on the grenade. Tom's head spun. He felt exhausted, but to stop was to die. The scorching sun bore down on him and he was drenched in sweat. A machine gun blazed away in the distance. It sounded like one of the Army's M60s. How he hoped the bullets hit their intended targets. Overhead, he watched as an A-1E Skyraider, an old and slow Korean War vintage aircraft, poured ordnance of many kinds, bombs, napalm, and machine gun rounds, accurately and precisely on the nearby foe.

Most definitely, they'd found the enemy, as ordered, and now they were in a hellish fight for their very lives. Tom desperately searched for his gun, but it was nowhere in sight. He saw another

M16 near Bill's lifeless remains, and he crawled to it. On close examination, he found it to be inoperable and useless. He saw movement nearby and another GI he did not know, crawled his way. His movement brought fire from the enemy. Tom heard a sound like a canoe paddle smacking mud, but it was the sound a bullet makes when it strikes human flesh. A painful curse came from the other man's mouth. Tom saw the man was hit in the hip. A white, jagged bone stuck out of the ugly wound. Tom crawled to him and applied first aid to stop or slow the bleeding, which he hoped would keep the wounded man out of shock. Tom noted the name Lindeman on the shirt. The man cursed some more, and then he said, "I'll be all right. Which way to the band-aid?"

"You mean the medic?"

"Yeah."

Carefully, Tom raised his head and took a quick look. He dropped back down as bullets whizzed around him. "It's over there," and Tom pointed with his finger. "Thanks," he said and crawled off in that direction.

"You're welcome," replied Tom. For a quick moment, all seemed surreal. Here they were on a battlefield with men dying all around them, and two men had spoken a common courtesy to each other among all the destruction.

As the other man crawled off toward the aid station, Tom laid on the ground and closed his eyes while bullets whizzed barely over his head. He opened his eyes and wiped the dirt from his face. Not five feet away, lay an M-16. The other man may have dropped it, or it may have been there for some time before he noticed it, but it was there like a forgotten gift. Tom crawled over and grabbed it with his outstretched arm. He pulled it near him and saw it was operable and still had a full clip. There was also ammo laying near him that someone had dropped. He grabbed it up. How he wished he had his entrenching tool, but with the amount of heavy fire overhead, he would probably be dead if he rose up to dig. Whenever he saw movement in the bush, he fired and often saw something drop. Fortunately, he still had his canteen and sipped from it occasionally. The water was so good. If he moved, he drew fire. He'd stay behind the fallen tree until conditions improved, or he was ordered elsewhere.

He remained there for the longest time. He could hear the Hueys coming in when the battle seemed to lull a bit. Still, they had to run a gauntlet of enemy fire again and again. They landed hot with supplies and loaded the wounded in record speed, reducing their exposure on the ground. Death was everywhere.

Brave men, risking their lives for us. One hot round hitting the ammo they brought would turn them into a great burst of sunshine followed by a cloud of dark smoke.

Around Landing Zone X-Ray, a series of loud explosions occurred. The enemy probed for a weak spot, an opening, a wedge through the thin line of soldiers defending the vital landing zone. The enemy was eager to kill them all and hungered to do so.

In the afternoon, the raging battle faded to sporadic firing. Some sense of order fell around the landing zone. Choppers came and went with little resistance. Night operations were set up with artillery and mortars around the perimeter. Tom found other members of his unit, among them Chris Benally, and helped set up a jury-rigged little black-out tent with ponchos to serve as a lighted place where they could work on the wounded. After fighting to survive earlier, they now had enough ammo, and morphine and bandages.

A late, lone chopper flew into LZ X-Ray. Shortly afterward, artillery began to fall on a nearby hillside. Men in the Huey had spotted hundreds of little, twinkling lights heading for the landing zone. The North Vietnamese were coming. Around midnight, a massive explosion occurred on a mountain to the right of X-Ray. It was a restless night for all units now on one hundred percent alert. A full moon, a Hunter's Moon, rose around twenty-three hundred hours in the clear sky, and its brightness cast dim shadows that night. Tom was called to help the medics. Casualties were bleeding to death faster than new blood could be put in them. Caution was thrown to the wind, and patients were given four intravenous tubes at once with four corpsmen, one being Tom, squeezing the blood bags as hard as possible. He watched as many men, getting the blood, shivered and quaked as so much cold blood entered their bodies.

Snipers harassed the moonlit men. They located one sniper hidden in the top of a palm tree. Repeated firing into the treetop finally found the mark, but not before five men died, and an equal number were wounded.

Tom was relieved of his duties in the makeshift hospital and was sent back to guard the perimeter. He found himself next to Chris Benally. Somehow, they had both escaped with only scratches and scrapes. About three-hundred hours, rushing sounds were heard by the men in LZ X-Ray. Someone shot up several illumination flares that made the night appear like the day. The inside of the perimeter had numerous North Vietnamese who had stealthily advanced in the darkness. Every soldier's gun opened up on them. Tom's gun was on automatic, and he saw many of the enemy fall from his fire; one was nearly cut in half from the steady stream of bullets. After fifteen minutes, it was all over. By the light of the last flares, they saw North Vietnamese dragging their dead and wounded into the thick jungle.

First light revealed dozens of khaki-clad enemy dead scattered around the landing zone. Tom looked at Chris and said wearily, "Well, we made it through the night."

Chris nodded, "Yeah, we did, but a lot of men didn't. We may not see the morning tomorrow. Have you thought any more about what I told you about Jesus and salvation? Where will you be going if we die out here on this battlefield?"

Tom said, "It was interesting stuff you said. Glad you believe it. I'll have to think about it some more."

Chris nodded his head knowingly. "I'm glad you're thinking. They are trying to kill us, and I don't think I'd take my time making a decision. Our time could run out today just like it did for so many others on both sides today."

Tom smiled the first smile he had smiled in a day. "Thanks for thinking of me, brother." He reached his hand out to shake the big Indian's hand, but once Chris had Tom's hand, he pulled Tom close in a bear hug and said, "We are a band of brothers baptized in blood and fire. May the Lord grant us mercy to live to tomorrow, or lead us by His nail-scarred hands home."

"Amen," said Tom.

"Hey, you two! Get down! There's still snipers out there," came a phantom voice from somewhere nearby.

The two men dropped to the ground as a bullet whizzed by above them, where their heads had just been. Tom said, "Forgot where I was for a minute."

"Me too," said Chris. "Glad someone reminded us in the nick of time."

"Yeah," replied Tom. "Another brother."

"Yeah," repeated Chris. "Another brother."

The two men laid on the dirt, and both fell asleep exhausted. A few minutes later, an explosion shattered their sleep. Someone to the left was screaming, "They're coming, Sarge! A lot of them. Get ready!"

The two men woke with a start. Adrenaline shot through their bodies. This was it. *They're coming!*

Tom took a quick look over the fallen tree and saw the enemy advancing. Their helmets had nets on them, and they had stuck grass in the netting. They looked almost like short trees. There were about 50, and Tom and Chris put their guns on the fallen tree and began to fire with the weapons on automatic. An M79 grenade launcher opened up down the line. Others nearby opened up mowing down many of the enemy, but their return fire was whittling down the thin line of the American boys. The enemy dropped back and came again. The results were the same; many dead for the North Vietnamese, but the American line kept getting thinner too.

The fighting stopped except for an occasional shot here and there. From behind them, two hunched men carrying a machine gun and boxes of ammo came running in. They hid behind the fallen tree, too.

The larger of the two said, "Sarge wants you two to head for the center. Choppers are coming in with ammo and carrying out the wounded and dead. He needs you two on the double."

Tom nodded that he understood, and he heard Chris say, "Will do."

The two men half ran, half crawled, zigzag to make them less of a target, though shots rang out around them as they went to the middle of the LZ. As they reached the sarge, the first chopper was landing. His instructions were to quickly unload ammo and water and then reload the Huey with the wounded first and any dead if there was room.

That morning, helicopter after helicopter landed. Ammo disappeared when it hit the ground, and space where the dead and wounded were carried out by the last Huey, filled again with casualties. When the fighting was too hot for landings, Tom and Chris returned enemy fire from their positions, but most of the time, the Hueys came in through the firing. A giant of a man with "Too Tall" printed in white ink on his helmet expertly piloted the one. Whatever chopper came in, they did their seemingly endless job of loading and unloading.

A lull fell on the battle, and in came the helicopters. They'd no more than landed when all hell broke loose again. Mortars hit nearby, and bullets flew like angry hornets from a fallen nest. They unloaded water, ammo, and grenades from one with a very small pilot and, as quickly as possible, began to fill the cargo area with the wounded. They had just finished loading a large, unconscious man in when Tom felt a horrifying pain in his groin. He looked down to see shreds of his pants and lots of blood. **"I'm hit!"**

Chris took one look at the wound and began to help Tom into the Huey. A hand reached out and helped pull Tom in. He laid on his back in horrible pain. The air shook with noise and bullets. Chris shook as the rounds found their mark. "Help me!" he said to Tom and anyone who may hear. "Help me!"

Tom reached for Chris to pull him in, but he hurt so badly and only got him part way in. From somewhere behind, a big hand attached to a long arm reached forward, and with this help, Chris was pulled into the Huey. He fell on top of Tom, and they lay nose-to-nose and eye-to-eye. The chopper lifted off rapidly in a hail of bullets. Soon, it was out of range of ground fire and headed to the base camp twelve miles away.

The men, packed like cordwood, groaned in pain as the chopper flew toward its destination. Tom could feel Chris's warm blood draining on him. Still face-to-face, Chris raised his head and looked eye-to-eye at Tom and said through the pain, "Tom, I'm dying. I know it."

Tom said, "Hold on, Chris. We can make it." He said this as much to reassure himself as he did for Chris's benefit.

Chris slowly shook his head from side-to-side. "No, Tom, I ain't goin' to make it," he said. "You remember what I told you, and promise me this."

"What? What do you want me to promise to?"

"Do you promise?" asked Chris.

Tom nodded the best he could under the circumstances. "Yeah, I promise. What do you want me to do?"

"Go see my father and tell him I died in battle. It'll mean a lot to him. Promise you will."

"I promise," said Tom.

A little smile came to Chris's face, then his head dropped on Tom's shoulder and stayed there. Tom's shirt oozed with sweat and hot blood. His groin ached in pain. A tear rolled from his eye, followed by many more. He cried like he had not cried since he was a child. And then like a child, he fell asleep much the same as a dead man.

Chapter 9

"Hurry up! Get 'em out of that chopper. And get that ammo ready to go," yelled Big Tony.

It was organized confusion around the MASH unit as the choppers landed with their grim cargos. Grunts with bloody hands and bloody clothes untangled the casualties in the choppers. Quickly and not gently, they removed the human cargo. They put the men on gurneys and took them to triage where Staff Sergeant Chief Medical NCO "Big Tony" separated them into three groups: dead and beyond hope, salvageable and in need of immediate attention, and salvageable and can wait for treatment. Usually, a doctor did this, but today was no usual day. They were short of doctors. Two were sick with malaria, and one was out with appendicitis. It was up to Big Tony to fill in the slack.

When the last wounded man was removed from the chopper, Big Tony threw a bucket of water in the cargo area to wash away the slippery blood that covered it.

"Now, get that ammo in the Huey! Those guys are dying out there without it," screamed Big Tony. He was a man who could out cuss and out growl a roomful of drill sergeants any day when he wanted to, which wasn't often necessary. When Big Tony spoke, men moved in a hurry. The chopper was soon full, lifted off, and headed back to the battle. It had been doing this all day.

Big Tony went around inspecting the casualties for the severity of their wounds. He decided who went next to the surgeons and treatment. Literally, he held the lives of many men in his hands.

If you were too far gone from waiting, you went to the first group to die and another man moved to the head of the line for treatment. As he walked around examining the wounded, a hand reached out and grabbed him. He looked down at the man who stopped him. Big Tony saw his name was Kenney, in spite of the blood and dirt covering his shirt. "Is he gonna survive?" the wounded man asked.

"Is who gonna survive?" asked Big Tony.

"My friend, the big Indian. Is he gonna make it?"

Big Tony looked into the wounded man's face and immediately knew who he was asking about. The big Indian's body was among the dead taken from the airships, lying on the ground, and waiting for processing. Big Tony lied as he had to so many GIs who'd asked the same question. "He'll be all right. You need to take care and worry about yourself. We'll take care of him." Big Tony patted the man's hand and lied again, "He'll be all right." Then he raised his head and yelled out to someone, "Private Smith, get your ass over here and start an IV in this man, lots of happy juice for him."

"Sorry, Sarge," medic Smith yelled back. "Still busy on this one. Can you get someone else?"

Big Tony grumbled some strong profanity under his breath. Yes, he would get it, but he was not going to like it. He got the IV and a bag containing morphine, found a good vein in the arm of the blood-covered soldier, inserted the IV, and began the flow. Big Tony yelled, "Need blood here," and a man nearby brought a bag and an IV. Big Tony inserted this IV in the other arm and began the blood flow.

Private Smith came over and was examining the wound. He reached down, pulled at something, and blood squirted everywhere. "What the hell are you doin'?" screamed Big Tony.

"I pulled a stick out of his leg," replied Private Smith.

"You idiot! It was in his femoral artery! He'll bleed to death!" Big Tony pushed the startled man away and put his hand over the wound to stop the blood squirting. "I should put you on report. Get out of my sight! ***Now!***"

Private Smith nearly ran from the angry Sergeant. Big Tony shook his head. *Moron. He could have killed this man if I hadn't been here. If the enemy doesn't kill 'em, our own stupid people will.* He stopped the bleeding and looked again at the wounds to the man's groin and legs. It was worse than his first hasty assessment had determined. The man would survive, but he needed more help than was available at this MASH unit. The 8th Field Hospital in Nha Trang had doctors and facilities for this kind of wound. That was where he was going. "Private Smith," he yelled. "Come here. This man needs transported to the big hospital. Do you think you can help me without tripping over your own feet and dropping this poor soldier?"

"Yes, sir," he yelled. "Coming right up, sir."

Private Smith arrived, and the two men quickly picked up the stretcher. They moved him to the group waiting for evac. Soon, he'd be heading for the hospital on the coast. Big Tony walked away and spoke to Private Smith. "Smith," he said, "keep up the good work. Anyone can make a stupid mistake. Learn from it and don't ever do that again. Understand?"

"Yes, sir. Thank you, sir."

Private Smith continued back to the triage area. Big Tony looked at the carnage around him and shook his head. *If there was a god, how could he let horrors like this happen?* He sighed heavily. *And if there is a god, please be with the man on the stretcher me and Smith just carried over there. He's sure gonna need your help now, and in the future.* And then he moved on to the wounded, checking who was savable and who wasn't. War was hell. Only the dead have seen the last of it.

Chapter 10

Oh, my head hurts. Through the blur, Tom looked around. *Where am I?* Nothing seemed familiar. He was on a bed in a hospital somewhere and had an IV was in his wrist. *But what am I doing here?* He looked around the room and saw other men in hospital beds. Slowly, it came back. Vietnam. The battle. Getting hit. At triage. And now he was here, wherever here was. He tried to move, and intense pain hit below his waist. ***"Awhh!"*** He screamed, and a nurse appeared from somewhere.

"Well, you finally woke up," she sharply. 'Thought we had another Rip Van Winkle in the ward. Some of you guys sleep for days. Trauma and some crazy anesthesia will do that."

Tom looked at the nurse and groaned, "Nurse, who are you, and where am I?"

"I'm one of the nurses on this ward. The name's Lt. Jackson, Lt. Marg Jackson, but most people call me, Nurse Jackson. And the answer to the second question is, you're at the 8th Field Hospital in Nha Trang in the vacation capital of the world, South Vietnam."

Tom grunted. "Looks like this vacation took a turn for the worse, and I had too much fun. How bad is it?"

"I'll get the doctor. He wanted to talk with you when you awoke. Be right back."

"I'm not going anywhere," he lamented to her backside as she turned and briskly walked away.

A short time later, the doctor and nurse walked up to Tom's bed. "Well, Private Kenney, I'm Dr. Kalidas. I see you're no longer asleep, and I bet you have questions. I'll answer all I can."

Tom said without enthusiasm, "I remember the battle and getting hit. Guess the army got me here while I was knocked out and patched me up as best they could."

The doctor said, "You're very fortunate to be alive. Twenty years ago, your wounds would have been fatal."

"Just how bad is it, doctor?" Tom asked.

"Compared to a lot of what I have seen here, you're lucky. This hospital holds a little over one hundred, and most would gladly change places with you."

Tom let out a deep sigh. "When you put it that way, it sounds much better, but what's wrong with me? I feel pain in my legs and lower trunk. What happened?"

The doctor looked at the nurse and then spoke. "From what we can figure out, you were hit by a bullet, shrapnel, flying debris, or all three. The best news is, you will recover and have the ability to live to an old age if the fates allow."

"That's good," said Tom, "but what's the bad news?"

"The bad news," repeated the doctor. "The bad news is, you nearly died. If not for someone's actions, you would have bled to death. Someone patched up a hole in your femoral artery somewhere between the battle and when you got here. It was expert work. Whoever did this, saved your life."

"Any more bad news?"

With a straight face showing no emotion, the doctor said, "You lost one of your testicles. Whatever hit you took it off and damaged the other. I was able to save the second and reattach the damaged ducts. You'll look a little different in the manhood department from what you were, but with our corrective surgery, you should have no problem having a family." Tom sighed. The doctor continued, "You had some shrapnel or debris in your legs and trunk, which we removed. How much these spots will scar is unknown, but we should know by the time you leave here."

Tom asked, "And how long will that be?"

"Two to three weeks if all goes well, and the swelling goes down."

The nurse next to the doctor suppressed a snicker. The doctor looked at her questioningly and realized what he had said. He smiled and said to Tom, "The swelling in your legs from the dirty intruders that is. Your favorite organ should be able to swell and function quite normally and effectively."

"Well," said Tom. "That's certainly good to know."

"I better be going. I need to check on some others upstairs. Private Kenney, I'll be around each day checking on your progress, and if you have more questions, please ask. See you then." He turned and hastily left the large hospital room.

When he was out of sight, the nurse let the snicker out and said, "The doc's somewhat of a no-nonsense, straight-laced guy with some things, but there's no one here who questions his surgical skills. I was there assisting as he put your broken parts back together. You were in good hands."

"Seems like I've been in lots of good hands lately," Tom and smiled.

The nurse laughed. “It’s good you haven’t lost your sense of humor. It will help with your recovery.” She got near Tom’s bed and whispered in his ear, “Soldier, as a nurse of twenty years, I’ve seen it all including yours up close and personal. You’re going to be all right, and I think, keep a wife very happy when you fulfill your lovemaking abilities with that bad boy.”

Tom was a little shocked to hear her frankness with him, but also pleased and relieved.

The nurse drew away from Tom and said, “Just like the doctor, I have others I need to see. I’ll check on you later. Anything else you need before I go?”

Tom thought for a moment and asked, “Yes, I was with a friend, Private Chris Benally, in the battle. He got hit bad. Could you check and see how he’s doing?”

“Be glad to, soldier. I’ll get on the horn and see. It may take a while, but I’ll get you an answer.”

“Thanks,” Tom said. “I’m thankful there are still angels like you.”

She smiled. “You’re welcome. I’ll check about your friend, Private Benally, and give you the information when it comes in. Bye.” And she was off to her other duties.

Tom suddenly felt very tired. He was alive and in good hands. As he thought about that, he drifted off to sleep.

One week later

Tom sat on a bench and looked out of the hospital window towards the ocean. Somewhere, many thousands of miles away across a vast ocean and a continent was home, and he wished he could be there. He thought of the guys who'd been here and been sent back to their units. The doctors said he'd be back with the other soldiers after a month of recovery. A few short months ago, when he was in school, if someone had told him all that would happen to him from then until now, he'd have said them they were nuts. But here he was. How he wanted to go home to the USA. He let out a sigh and looked up to see Dr. Kalidas and Nurse Jackson coming his way.

They walked up to him. "Private. Kenney, we've been looking for you. We have news that concerns you."

Tom looked at them and said, "Okay, don't keep me in suspense. What's the news? How soon? When?"

The nurse and the doctor traded glances. The doctor spoke first. "An Army board has been looking at your situation and made a decision based on finding out about two things."

"And what's that?" asked Tom.

"The two are related to keeping you in the Army. Number 1, the Army is concerned about a report they received on your father's health. His wife, your mother, has been dead for some time, and you are the only close relative. They're concerned about who will care for him as his Parkinson's progresses." He paused. "And Number 2, because of your injury and you being the only one to carry on the family name, they're concerned if they send you back into action, a similar injury will extinguish the family line. Because of these two things, the board recommended an honorable discharge with full benefits. You're to be discharged as soon as you are well enough to leave."

Tom said nothing. He looked stunned and remained mute.

"You did hear me, Private Kenney? You're going home."

Tom looked at both of them. “Yes, I heard you. I just can’t believe it. Home and soon. I thought for sure they were sending me back to my unit.”

Nurse Jackson spoke, “I have some news too. It’s about your friend, Private Benally. I’m sorry; he didn’t make it.”

Tom murmured, “I know. I could feel it in my heart. I knew he was gone.”

“We’re sorry about your friend,” she said, “but glad you’re going home.”

“Life’s not fair,” said Tom. “It should have been me and not Chris. Why? Why am I still here?”

Nurse Jackson replied, “No, life’s not fair, and neither you nor all the doctors or nurses in the world can make it so, as much as we’d like to. You just have to go on and try to make some sense of it.” She stopped. “There’s a hundred people in this hospital that wish those discharge orders were for them. Consider yourself lucky. You survived it and will live to tell about it. Don’t try to understand everything. Just get yourself healed up and go back to where you were and make a life of it. Isn’t that what your friend would want you to do?”

“Guess you’re right. It’s so much to digest. Gonna take a while to get used to being a civilian again,” said Tom.

“Let’s leave the young man to his thoughts,” the nurse said to the doctor. “If I were in your shoes, I’d want to be alone to think.”

Tom smiled, “Nurse Jackson, you’ve known me for only a short time, and already you can read my thoughts. Thank you two for all you’ve done for me. I don’t know how I can repay you.”

"Go lead a good and long life. That's payment enough," said the doctor, and the nurse nodded her head in agreement. They walked away, leaving Tom to his thoughts.

Home and my dad. Will it all be the same? Somehow, after what I've been through, it will be the same, only different. And what of the promise I made to a dying man? What can I say to Chris Benally's father? Nothing can bring Chris back. What could I possibly say to him to bring him comfort?

Chapter 11

Tom walked through the airport terminal in San Francisco. It marked the start of his grand plan to see the country on the way home. California was a welcome change from the heat and stench of Vietnam. He'd already been clued in that some may not give him a welcome home if they knew he was a GI returning from the war zone. The Army would ship what little possessions he had home to West Virginia for him. He wanted to see the city, but first, there were some things he wanted to do. At the airport, he checked out what public transportation available. Tom saw he'd have more options once he got into town. He especially wanted to ride the cable cars once there, but that would have to wait, so he took the bus from the airport to the downtown area.

So many new things had entered the country boy's life since he'd made that crazy decision to go with Johnny joy riding. And now he was heading to a place he'd only heard about. Tom hoped the city would like up to the hype, and he wouldn't be disappointed. California didn't look like West Virginia or Vietnam for that matter, either.

There weren't too many passengers riding on that Saturday morning. The bus rolled along the dark blue waters of San Francisco Bay. Houses side by side took up every available spot of land, and multilane highways occupied what little was left. The air was arid, unlike Vietnam, where it felt like an overheated steam bath. Tom noted the mountain between him and the ocean. White fog rolled over the green hilltop, but it quickly dissipated as it went down the steep slope. In a short time, the bus rolled to a stop in an area called the Embarcadero, which another passenger told him was Spanish for the wharf. Today was his day to see as much of this compact city as possible. He hopped another bus that took him to Fisherman's Wharf. From a map he picked up at the airport, he had developed a plan for his day in the city by the bay.

Tom found Fisherman's interesting, but the air off the bay, chilly. It was quite a shock to his system after sweltering Vietnam. He looked across the choppy, foreboding waters to Alcatraz. Not too long ago, some of America's most notorious criminals were confined doing hard times on The Rock, as that island was known. Nearby were plenty of places to buy tourist items, lots of restaurants, and attractions. Sea lions and seals resting on some of the floating docks and made lots of noise. Several large Navy ships were docked in the area, and he could see the Golden Gate Bridge. He was surprised to see it was painted a burnt red, not gold.

Tom walked down Jefferson Street to Hyde Street and hopped a cable car. He wasn't sure where it would take him, but a sense of adventure propelled him forward. After getting off at the Cable Car Barn and Museum, the young man toured the facility. He found it hard to believe how old this technology was and how well it still worked. After the tour, he walked some five blocks to nearby Chinatown. He saw numerous shops selling Chinese themed touristy items, several ethnic grocery stores with strange smells coming from inside and plucked ducks hanging out front, the typical Chinese restaurants, and numerous drug/herbal stores selling everything from horny goat weed to Hershey chocolate, and eaches novelty beckoned him in. Tom walked down the street, and as he neared a corner, loud noises like gunfire erupted. Instinctively, he dropped to the ground and crawled for cover. He looked up to see people with slanted eyes staring down at him. For a few seconds, images of the battle of Ia Drang Valley filled his head, and as quickly as it came, it was over. Some kids had set off a string of firecrackers. Tom picked himself up off the sidewalk and looked at the curious crowd he'd attracted. His stomach churned, and he swiftly left this uncomfortable place. On a corner, he passed a brick Catholic church with a square steeple, a clock on each side, and the words, 'Redeem the times for the days are evil,' from the book of Ephesians. *How appropriate considering what I've seen lately.*

He hopped another trolley, and six short blocks later, it stopped. An old lady in a Ford Falcon had T-boned a cable car up ahead, and no one was going anywhere on this route soon. After about ten minutes, a city bus stopped, and the driver yelled for the trolley passengers to get on. Everyone piled out, and Tom got the last seat open. The fear he felt before was now just a lingering, troubling memory. The bus continued to make its rounds. Few people got off, and many more got on. The aisles were full of standing people, and the overloaded bus now bottomed out at each intersection. Each time it hit, Tom wondered if anything would be left of the underside of the vehicle, but the driver went on adding still more passengers until it was as full as a sardine can. A young couple dressed like hippies got on the bus, and the young woman was very pregnant. She stood in front of Tom and held one hand onto the strap hanging from the ceiling and cradled her belly with the other. Tom offered her his seat. She looked questioningly at the young man with her who nodded his approval. Tom got up, and the young man helped his awkward companion into the seat.

She looked up at Tom. "Thank you. You don't know how much I was hoping for a gentleman to be on this bus."

The young man spoke to Tom, "My name is Pat, but most people call me Grizzly because of my hair and beard. And that's Joyce, but she likes to be called Little Flower."

"Well, hi, Grizzly and Little Flower. My name is Tom, but most people just call me Tom." He smiled at that as did the two hippies.

"What are you doing in San Francisco?" asked Grizzly.

"I just got a medical discharge from the Army. I was in Vietnam."

The two looked at Tom uneasy. "The war isn't too popular around here, and neither are GIs. It'd be better if you kept that to yourself. Some are downright hostile to the military in this left-of-center town," advised Grizzly.

Tom said, "So I've heard." He was still a little surprised. How could anyone not respect a person who was only doing what his country asked? He kept these thoughts to himself and just nodded that he got the picture. He asked them, "What about you? What are you doing here?"

Grizzly said, "Why, this is San Francisco, the city of peace, love, and tranquility. Good vibes, man, good vibes."

Tom laughed. "Yeah, I can see the love part." He looked down at Joyce's swollen belly. "Looks like the two of you have been doing your part at doin' the making love part."

They smiled. "Yeah," said Grizzly. "That we have. That we have. We're gonna be parents, so we got to give up this hippie stuff and go straight. My dad has a job lined up for me in his entertainment business when we get to Pittsburgh, but I need money to get us there. Hey, you interested in a VW microbus? I'm so broke now I can't put gas in it. I'll give you a good price. I need bread for plane tickets to get us home quick."

"Bread? You need bread?" asked Tom.

"Money. I need money. You know, bread."

"Okay, got yeah. I'm not used to the lingo here in this part of town."

They talked a while longer about it. Tom said he might be interested if the price was right. The bus continued through the hilly city. The trio got off near Nob Hill and walked about a block to where the microbus was parked. It had a big peace sign on the front under the two-piece windshield and psychedelic designs and colors that would have made Peter Max proud covered the sides and back. The inside was pristinely clean and was set up to be a camper. It had a bed/couch, a small heater, a stove, and a sink. The 'bathroom' was a bucket with a toilet seat on top and cat litter in the bottom.

"Not gonna miss poopin' and peein' in that bucket," said Grizzly. "We lived in this thing for two years and saw a whole lot of the USA in it. My grandfather died some time back and left me money. I think he wanted me to go to college, but I bought this, and we used the rest to live on for two years. Guess it's time to face reality and go home. Plus, I got no real friends here. We quit doin' drugs when we found out she was pregnant. When we quit, all our 'friends' drifted away. It seems all we had in common was weed and drugs. We're ready to go home."

Tom looked the VW microbus over. He didn't really care what the outside looked like. The vehicle appeared in excellent shape mechanically. It had to work out well for his adventure going home across the United States. The two men haggled a little over the price and finally came to a price with which they could both live. Grizzly found the title to the vehicle in the glove box and signed it over to Tom. He drove them to a thrift store where they purchased some suitcases and two backpacks. The couple filled these up with their meager belongings. Anything that wouldn't fit or any things they didn't want now was left for Tom to use or dispose of. After this, Tom drove them to the airport by the bay. The couple got out, took their items, wished Tom the best of luck as he did them, and then disappeared into the large terminal.

Tom drove a few short miles to one of the parks with the colossal coastal redwoods. He couldn't believe trees could grow that tall. Trees in the eastern Appalachians could get big. He'd seen a few huge old trees there now and had seen pictures in the old book, "Tumult on the Mountain," of trees from the virgin forests the East, but the large trees were cut down one hundred years ago. He looked up and up and up at the redwoods that seemed to touch the very face of God and felt a sense of awe and also his own insignificance. They were so gigantic, and he felt so small. A few lay on their sides. Even the mighty could fall. Branches still green lay scattered on the ground. Even these giants weren't immune from the storms of life.

He got back in the VW microbus. It was running very well. Hippie Pat had taken excellent care of the vehicle. Tom remembered his promise to Chris about delivering Chris's last words to the dead friend's father. Oh, how he dreaded the thought of completing that task. Would he do it or not? The question kept going through his mind, and his stomach churned when he thought about it. Images of the battle in the Ia Drang Valley flooded his head. He mouthed the words, "God help me," as he sat in the vehicle and stared glassy-eyed through the divided glass windshield. Could he really complete this errand or not? "God help me," he whispered again.

After what seemed an eternity, Tom's mind cleared. Whether he delivered the message or not, he had to get home. He wanted to see Yosemite National Park, but this being winter, he feared snows in the Sierra Nevada Mountains that would close the mountain passes. So, he chose to head to southern California. Los Angeles he heard was a vast concrete jungle, and he wasn't going there. He continued to drive until he found himself in Pismo Beach. Tom pulled into a parking lot high on a cliff overlooking the Pacific

Ocean as the sun set into the waters. It was so peaceful here, but visions of the troubles on the other side of the vast ocean troubled Tom. And he was drained. It had been a very long day. Even though the parking lot was lighted, he was still able to see the full moon up above. It reminded him of the Hunter's Moon he had seen on the nights of the terrible battle. He used a portable toilet located near the microbus that needed cleaning. It was rather ripe and odorous. Fortunately, the wind was blowing the unpleasant smells inland away from the vehicle. Tom hopped back in the microbus, pulled out the bed, and was soon asleep.

***

Three hours later

What the ...? Tom woke with a start.

"You in the van. Open up, **Now!"** came a gruff voice outside.

Tom looked through the windows at a large man in a blue uniform wearing a Smoky the Bear type hat. "Just give me a second officer," Tom said. He opened the side door and stared at the cop with his sleepy eyes. "Is there a problem, sir?"

The cop looked at Tom, and there was an element of surprise on his face. "There's no sleeping here. You gotta move now."

"Sorry, sir. Didn't know it wasn't allowed." Tom looked at the policeman and asked, "Something wrong, officer?"

The cop looked carefully at Tom. "You weren't what I expected. I saw the psychedelic paint job and expected a bunch of stoned-out hippies. With that crew cut, you look more like a GI."

"I just got discharged from the Army. Bought this van from a hippie up in San Francisco. I'm gonna see the country on my way back home to West Virginia."

"I was in Richmond once. Pretty state."

"That's in Virginia, not West Virginia. Virginia is pretty, but I think West Virginia is prettier, though I'm a bit prejudiced about my home state."

"Sorry about that. Where did they have you?"

"Vietnam."

The cop whistled through his teeth. "Hell of a place. I wouldn't give two cents for the whole place, North and South. Got a brother in the Air Force. He's in Da Nang and can't wait to get home. Hey, forget I said this, but I'm going to look the other way and let you stay here for the night. We've had some trouble with dopers and gangs breaking into vehicles in the area, so I'm gonna pass by when I'm out patrolling and make sure you are okay. How 'bout that?"

"Well, thanks. I appreciate that, sir."

"And quit calling me, sir. No need for that, but when you did, I could tell you were brought up right or were a GI, maybe both. Either way, I could see you weren't gonna be a problem for me. Have yourself a restful night, and sorry for the bother. I need to get back on my rounds. Take care and have a good trip back to Virginia, oops, I mean West Virginia."

"Thanks sir, and 'Go Mountaineers'."

The cop shook his head. "Sir," he muttered and shook his head again. "Have a good night."

Tom was soon back to sleep. He slept the rest of the night away peacefully, and the cop did swing by several times just as he said he would. Tom woke at sunrise the next morning. He fixed some of the food the couple had left in the refrigerator, but he did smell it first. Today, he'd head for Las Vegas. There, he would have to decide to go south of the Grand Canyon and later deliver Chris's last words to his father or drive north through Utah and skip the meeting altogether. Which way would he go? He sighed. *God, please help me.*

Chapter 12

"Back in the saddle again," came the words from the radio in the VW microbus. Tom had found an oldies station and was listening to Gene Autry and other cowboy singers as he sped away from Las Vegas. The trip to the city hadn't been what he had expected. He found the Joshua trees along the highway interesting, but overall, the desert had been stark and somewhat monotonous. It was bleak and barren with lots of rocks and a few cacti that seemed to be dying. At a gas station where he had stopped for fuel and a snack, he'd seen some postcards of the desert in bloom. The pictures were beautiful. They must have been taken in the spring. Tom wished he could be there to see it like that, but right now, the desert was kind of depressing. Maybe Utah would be better, he hoped.

After much thought and soul searching, Tom realized he couldn't bring himself to face Chris Benally's father and tell him the story of his son's demise even if he had promised to do so. His stomach churned when his mind returned to thoughts of his denying Chris's dying request, but here he was heading north into Utah when he should be traveling south and then east across northern Arizona.

Las Vegas was a downer too for the country boy. The architecture of the many hotels was somewhat impressive, yet the glitter and glitz of the city failed to impress him overall. He especially liked the tall Stratosphere Hotel. How they made it look like a mirage puzzled and fascinated him, but the casinos of Freemont Street were a letdown. The billboards along the highway coming into town showed happy people full of life having fun in the gambling halls, but to him, the people there seemed anything but joyful. Everyone seemed consumed with what they were doing at the tables, whether it was Keno, Black Jack, or a variety of other games unknown to him.

It was no wonder why the alcohol needed to flow so freely. You'd have to be a little tipsy to stay here and endure this. He'd felt like yelling at them, "Get a life!" but figured that would only get him thrown out into the street. Some of the people looked beyond hope anyway. Their faces reminded him of people on drugs. And it seemed like every corner outside of the hotels and casinos had at least one working girl plying the oldest profession. He was happy to leave town earlier than he'd planned.

The highway to Utah went through more bleak desert before it found its way to the Virgin River, which the busy road followed. The river cut a deep canyon on its way to the Grand Canyon of the Colorado River. Near the river was a little life. He saw a few trees, mainly cottonwood, and some other low bushes and greenery with which he wasn't familiar. At least, it was a little green like back home.

Southern Utah near St. George was an improvement over where he'd left. The mountains surrounding the town had a few trees, and the valley where the small city sat at least had some scrubby vegetation. He noted that some of the homes had a few real trees around them. It seems like wherever people called home, they want some green trees around them for comfort. Even in barren Las Vegas, he'd noted this. He wondered what kind of effort was needed to keep them alive in that dry and thirsty land and what species could tolerate these challenging conditions. Man always seemed to desire to change his environment into something different.

A little north of the town of Washington, he turned onto State Route 9. It continued to follow the free-flowing Virgin River in a steep-walled valley. Soon, he was passing through the small touristy town of Springdale, the gateway to Zion National Park, his destination for the day. He stopped at the park campground and paid for a campsite for the night. The bathhouses were heated and he looked forward to a hot shower. The ranger at the campground took his money for the overnight stay and also for the park admission, and then gave him the needed passes. Tom drove the short distance to the park entrance at the foot of the deep valley through which the whitewater Virgin River flowed. In the park, the first thing he saw was a large stone arch that had caught his keen eyes. It was high off to the right, and most people would have missed it, but hunting in the wooded hills of West Virginia had made him aware of the importance of small details. It was one of the reasons; he'd ended up in the air infantry.

He drove on up the valley stopping many times. It had to be one of the most beautiful places on God's green Earth. No wonder the early settlers had called this Zion like the place where God's holy temple was located. The high sandstone walls reminded him of a cathedral with the sky for a roof. Early settlers had given the great monoliths names like The Three Patriarchs, East and West Temple, Great White Throne, and Cathedral Mountain. He parked the colorfully painted vehicle in a parking lot where the trail to Angels Landing started. It was a long steep ascent with many high drop-offs. At one point, they were on both sides of the narrow footpath. Even the country boy felt a twinge of fear as he continued his climb to the top. When Tom reached the top, he could see why they called this place Angels Landing. You could see forever from here, maybe even into the very face of this beautiful valley's Creator. He stayed there for a long while, basking in the beauty.

The walk down went faster, but he could feel the strain on his knees. Tom was glad for a chain to hold onto as he descended the steep trail. An older couple had stopped to rest on a crude bench. They asked him if the climb had been worth it. He emphatically told them it was, and they would regret it if, after coming this far, they didn't complete it. They thanked him, and he continued his walk down the trail. Ten minutes later, Tom came around a bend and saw a sight in the parking lot he didn't like. There were two armed rangers with a German Shepherd dog looking at his microbus. The dog was sitting and one ranger who Tom took to be his handler, was giving him a treat.

Tom walked up to the van as the rangers watched him suspiciously. "Is there a problem, officers?" he asked.

"This your van?" the taller of them asked.

"Yes, I bought it from a hippie couple down in San Francisco. I just got out of the Army after being in Vietnam. Thought I'd drive back to my home in West Virginia while I was still footloose-and-fancy-free and had the time." Tom stopped. "Is there a problem?"

"Yeah, the dog seems to think you got some dope in the van," said the shorter man, the dog's handler.

Tom's mouth dropped open, and his eyes grew wide. "If there's anything like that in there, it ain't mine, but the previous owners."

"Can we search it?" the tall man asked.

Reluctantly, Tom agreed. He opened the door, and the dog jumped in. He was all over the microbus sniffing everywhere and finding nothing. Finally, he hopped out of the vehicle, turned again, and sniffed at a small something on the floor by the door opening. He then sat down. The two rangers looked at each other. The tall one picked up what the dog had hit on. He held the small brown and round object up for Tom to see. "This, young man," he said flatly, "is a marijuana seed."

There was a long pause as the rangers let this sink in on Tom.

"Well, it ain't mine. I never mess with that stuff. Must have been the previous owners. I can show you the paperwork that proves I just bought it."

The two rangers again were silent and looked at the fearful Tom.

"That dog has the best nose I have ever seen. Most of them would have missed this in a closed-up vehicle, but not ole Deputy Dawg," said the handler.

The rangers were silent again and waited for a reaction from Tom.

"Like I said, it ain't mine."

The rangers waited for more, but Tom remained silent. Finally, after what seemed an eternity, the taller one spoke. "I believe you. You just don't look or seem the part. I've been around the pike a few times, and I don't take you for the kind of person that's a doper and a liar. The paint job on the van had me wondering, that and the California temporary tags. You may want to get it painted before long, so you don't get any more unwanted attention from the boys in blue."

Tom let out a sigh of relief. "Thank you, guys. For a moment, I wondered if I was going to jail for that seed those hippies left in the van. Guess I need to vacuum it out thoroughly from top to bottom before I go anywhere else."

"There won't be any need for further cleaning. If Deputy Dawg can't find it, it's not there. He is the best drug dog I have ever seen. The local dopers hate him," said the handler.

"Do you call him Deputy Dawg after the cartoon character?" asked Tom.

"Yup, it was either that or Rin Tin Tin. The boys down at the office took a vote, and Deputy Dawg won. Now, young man, you have a great time here at Zion. Sorry for the trouble and drive carefully on our mountain roads."

"Will do, officers," said Tom. "Thanks for the advice both on driving and the paint job. I'll try to have a great time here in the West before I go home. I knew there'd be some surprises, but I don't need anymore because of one seed."

The two men chuckled. "You have a nice day, and we'll be seeing you." With that, they walked over to the Chevy Suburban and opened the door. Deputy Dawg jumped in the back seat and sat looking eagerly. He was still in full work mode. The men got in, and soon the vehicle disappeared down the road. Tom let out a great sigh of relief. He'd heard the whistle of the bullet again, but somehow, it had missed him once more. He could only hope his luck held out.

He continued on up the park road that followed the river to the end and parked in the near-empty lot. A sign pointed to the Virgin River trail. He followed the footpath for about a half-mile feet until he came to a large sign placed where the trail and river became one. "Warning," it said in bold letters. "Trail is subject to flash floods. Do not enter during showers or when rain is expected. Even if it is not raining at this location, rainfall upstream can cause flooding here. Beware. Five people drowned when this happened in 1960."

Tom had no intention of walking in the frigid water at this time of year, but it looked like an exciting excursion in the summertime. The rock walls went straight up nearly 1,000 feet. It would be an exhilarating hike at a later date if he ever returned. He enjoyed the solitude at the trail end. It was now mid-afternoon, and the sun passed behind below the high valley walls. The days were short this time of year, and darkness wasn't far off. He turned around and was startled to see a mountain man standing behind him. He was clothed in animal skins and carried a rifle on his back along with a primitive backpack of sorts. The grizzly, bearded man looked at Tom and asked, "Sonny, can you tell me what month this is and what year?"

Tom was surprised by the question, so the mountain man repeated it. "Why, it's December of 1966," Tom said.

The man seemed puzzled. "December of 1966?" Tom nodded his head. The man rubbed his heavily bearded chin with his leathery hand. "December 1966. Why, I've lost a whole year somewhere." He said no more, walked away, and disappeared into a cottonwood thicket along the river.

Tom was stunned. First, there was the encounter with the lawmen and now this strange man. What else was in store for him before he had finished this adventure? He walked back to his microbus, but he never did see any more of the mountain man. As quickly and quietly as he'd come, he vanished like a ghost. Was he real or had Tom just imagined this? He tried to put those troubling thoughts behind him.

He enjoyed the drive down the road and stopped at the numerous parking spots that the Park Service had for the tourists. The valley had to be one of the most beautiful places on earth; he was certain. He hoped he could return someday, maybe with a wife and kids. This magnificent place would still be here when the time came. He hoped he would be. Life could be so short and end at any moment. How well he knew that.

Tom drove out of the park and stopped at a grocery store and a gas station in town. Food and fuel could be a long way apart in the vast American West. He found what he needed at the two stores, drove to his campsite, and fixed himself a small supper. After a much-needed and refreshing hot shower in the bathhouse, he walked back to the van and got ready for the night. It was going to be cold here in the mountains, and he was thankful for the warm sleeping bag the hippies left, and it looked in good condition, nearly new. He laid on the fold-down bed that doubled as a bench seat and stared at the microbus's ceiling. What a day it had been! He'd nearly been busted by the cops and had a strange encounter with the mountain man, all in this beautiful valley. *Wonder what tomorrow will bring? What other adventures would he have on his way home?* Ten short minutes later, he was asleep dreaming dreams he would never remember in the morning. There was no way he could have imagined in his wildest dreams.

Chapter 13

"Man, it's cold," Tom said out loud though there was no one else to hear him in the vehicle. His breath created a fog when he exhaled. It was daylight, but it would be sometime before the sun climbed over the mountain tops and shined in the valley.

He crawled out of the sleeping bag, dressed warmly, and began to fix a quick breakfast. Cereal with powdered milk would do, but he had to have some hot coffee. He'd found little plug-in heating coil devise the hippies left that worked well but could be a fire hazard if you forgot it. One thing he knew he didn't want was a fire in the microbus. This vehicle had to get him home and provide shelter on the way, and not burn him up like an overcooked hot dog. He'd first experience the scent of burning human flesh at the battle in Ia Drang valley, and it was something he hoped never to smell again, especially his own.

After his quick breakfast and a trip to the bathhouse, Tom was off on Utah Route 9 East. The road went up another steep-walled valley in the National Park. Rain had fallen overnight in this rocky land, and the heavy drops on the metal roof woke him up. The shower was short but intense, and he was soon back to sleep last night. With next to no soil to hold the moisture, streams of water flowed where usually there was none. Many waterfalls formed where if fell over the cliff edges. "Beautiful," Tom said to the windshield. "Wish I had someone with me to enjoy this sight." It was a treat that few people would ever see in this semi-desert part of Utah.

Near the head of the valley, the road went through a series of switchbacks to gain altitude before it entered a tunnel, but it was one like none Tom had ever seen. It had windows. The tunnel was barely inside of the mountainside, and the builders had cut holes that provided magnificent views of the valley outside.

He exited the tunnel and entered a wonderland like one he could never have imagined. The sun shined down on the land, and it looked like it had been sculptured and painted by the Master's hand. Rock formations of every kind and every color, some with many bands of colors, delighted his eyes. It was hard to drive and look at the same time. Tom stopped near a giant rock, almost a small white mountain utterly devoid of any soil. The whole cone-shaped monolith had lines running up and down completely covering it and made it look like a giant tic-tac-toe board. Tom loved his home in the East, but it had nothing like this. He knew he'd be leaving a little bit of his heart in Utah. If the rest of the West looked like this, he'd consider living here if not for family ties back home.

He saw a buffalo farm near where Route 9 intersected Route 89, and there, he turned left, which took him north on Route 89. For the next forty miles, he traveled up a long valley with majestic snow-covered mountains on both sides. Then, he took a right on Route 12 and was soon at Bryce Canyon National Park. Snow covered the ground in this high altitude park. A ranger at the entrance building informed him that the road crew was busy cleaning the roads and parking lots in the park and not to expect many areas cleared because the snowfall had been heavier in the higher elevations near the main road's end. Tom asked about the condition of other highways in the area. The ranger said he had heard Route 12 was clear all the way to Torrey, usually a two-hour drive if you didn't stop to sightsee on the beautiful ride, which most people do.

Tom drove the hippie microbus for about ten miles before he found a plowed parking lot. The snow was deep, and the road beyond remained cover. The snow crew had just finished this lot and was heading back down the road. *Guess this is all I'll see of Bryce*

Canyon today. He walked through the foot deep snow to the viewing area, and he stood in wonder at the beauty of the rock formations called hoodoos that seemed to go on forever. Again, he wished he had someone with whom to share this incredible sight.

For ten minutes, he stood awestruck before the cold wind brought him back to reality. He hurried back to the vehicle nearly slipping twice and turned the heater on high, but he'd discovered the heater on this air-cooled engine produced less far less heat than he'd have liked.

The road crew was working at a fast pace clearing the next lot, but Tom realized he'd already seen all that was open today. He drove down the park road, stopped at Utah Route 12, and turned right. It only took a few short miles before he knew this drive would be as beautiful as the ranger described, if not more so. The two-hour drive took him twice as long.

At Torrey, he took a right at the T-bone intersection with Route 24, and this road was just as scenic as the last. He stopped at a poke and plumb town named Hanksville for a burger at an all-in-one general store. The man behind the counter advised him to gas-up as it was a 'fer distance' to the next town. He did and continued east on the same highway that went through a rolling desert with little vegetation.

He saw a new wooden sign that said "Canyonlands National Park". While at Zion, he'd seen a poster in the visitor's building that said, "Visit Canyonlands NP, our newest National Park," and he thought he would. He was on no one else's schedule but his own.

The road he turned on was frozen dirt, which made his a little wary, but the snow was plowed from it. After about ten long miles of seeing nothing but scrubby desert, not even another vehicle, he wondered if he'd made the right choice. The road squeezed between two jagged rock walls and then widened, but soon the plowed road ended. No tracks led down the ever-narrowing lane, and Tom knew he'd go no further. The wind picked up, and it was starting to snow. He turned the microbus around carefully. Getting stuck here was not an opinion. Tom needed to get out of here before the ever-changing weather did just that. Some locals at the campground had warned him they had four seasons, and they could have all four any day of the year. "Oh boy," Tom said. " I got to go." He'd felt the fullness earlier, but chose to ignore it. *Why hadn't he gone at the last stop?* He had to pee badly, so he quickly pulled the vehicle to a halt. Tom walked about six feet to the edge of the road and made water. The wind blew stronger, and the snow fell harder. Down the way, the thundering sounds of a murderous war battle came, and then an air blast filled with stinging, blinding dirt from a massive, fiery explosion hit him. *Oh, God. It's the North Vietnam Regulars! RUN!!*

***

Where am I? Why do I hurt so? He laid on his belly. Painfully, he rolled on his side and sat up. It was dark, and several inches of new snow was on the ground. *I'm cold. How long had I been here, and where is here?* His head hurt, and he felt a small dried stream of blood on his forehead, and his body ached so. The snow no longer fell, and a half-moon played peekaboo with the passing clouds. Looking around, he saw he was in a steep-walled arroyo. Back home, it would have been known as a gully, and the long dry wash now held him. The walls were at least ten feet up. *No way I can climb the sides.* He had to find another way out.

With some effort, he stood upright. *Oh, my his aching body.* Tom stumbled at first, but with each step, he became steadier. He walked for what he guessed was 1,000 feet, in the twisting trench to where he found a small trickle of water entering the wash down a small ditch. Tom cupped his hand and got some water to drink. He was thirsty, and the cold water felt good going down his parched throat. *Probably got coyote pee or crap in it.* He'd rather risk worms and parasites than dying of thirst. His thirst now quenched, he looked up the ditch in the dim moonlight, and it appeared climbable. It was slippery, but he managed to get out of the arroyo. He found himself in a flat, scrubby area, but he had no idea where he was. Hills rose to both sides. *I'm lost. What options do I have?*

The hill to his right looked less steep and higher. Perhaps from there, he could tell where he was and, with luck, find some shelter. The hill was farther off than it appeared, but after walking for at least twenty minutes, he arrived at the base of the rise. In the dark, he made out an animal trace that ascended the hill. It had a few steep places that challenged Tom's weary body. He looked around from his elevated position but could see only more scrubby rolling desert that seemed to go on forever. Huge sandstone rocks rose from the hill. Tom continued to climb. He came around a bend, and sitting on a rock outcropping no more than ten feet away from Tom, was a mountain lion. Startled, he backed away from the big growling cat that had its ears back and teeth showing. The cat followed him as he continued to back away. Tom never took his eyes off of the cat. Tom felt something hard and solid at his back. In his attempt to escape, he'd backed himself into a rocky corner. He was trapped. The big cat continued to approach ever growing closer and still looking like the predator the creature was. It stopped within six feet of the terrified man and continued to growl menacingly.

"Here, Kitty, Kitty," came a voice from somewhere. Tom questioned if he was hallucinating. This night had been unreal.

"Here, Kitty, Kitty," the voice repeated. The big cat quit snarling and looked around. Out of the darkness, a grizzly, roughly dressed man appeared. He looked at Tom, and his smile revealed missing teeth.

"Is my kitty frightening you? She's nothing but a big pussy cat, aren't you, Susie?" The big cat quit her growling and snarling.

She walked over to the raggedy man, and lovingly rubbed his leg. He dropped his hand to her head and gently began stroking it. He looked at Tom and spoke, "She's a good kitty. You needn't worry about her now. She knows you're not a threat to me. She's been the best friend this old man has ever had. Now, young man, do you want to stay out here in the cold and freeze to death or come to the warmth of my cabin? It's up to you. The animals will take care of disposing of your body if you choose not to. What do you say?"

Tom was short on options. Somehow, he found his voice, "Okay."

The big cat led the trio up the path in the pale moonlight. By Tom's reckoning, they'd walked about a country half-mile between various large rock formations and evergreen trees, probably some species of juniper. They rounded a blind bend, and Tom caught a whiff of smoke. "Almost there," he heard the man say.

Tom thought he saw a small light near the bottom of the cliff they were approaching. *Yes*, he was sure of it. He could see a dugout cabin that stood no more than three feet high and maybe twelve feet by twelve feet square. It would be tight for the three of them, but at least they'd be out of the cold and wind. The man walked to the cabin and stepped down a couple of crude steps to the weathered wooden door. He opened it a little and said, "Ready, Kitty?" The big cat snarled, walked away from the cabin, squatted down, and began to pee. "Oh yeah, forgot about that." When the big she-cat finished, she went to the cabin and walked in like she owned the place.

"How about you? You got to go, too?"

"Tom nodded and walked away from the cabin. The old man went into the structure.

Strange. That old guy must have a good bladder. Men his age usually got to go all the time. Tom took care of his business and entered the cabin. The big cat was in one corner of the cabin laying down in what seemed to be her personal space. The old man ran the wick up in a dim lantern, and light filled the room. It was spartan at best, but much better than being outside. A small homemade stove provided heat, and a teapot that had a little steam coming out of it sat on the flat top. The man was short, about five feet five inches, and had a long scar running down his left cheek. "The name's Gerald. You already met my cat Susie, also known as Kitty. We'd like you to be our guest tonight at our humble abode."

"I accept your generous offer," Tom said," but would you answer two questions? That cat will remain friendly, won't she, and just who are you?" The old guy smiled, revealing several missing teeth. "Don't worry about Kitty. She likes you. She told me that. And like I told you, my name is Gerald. Let's fill in the details about who we are and why we are here in the morning. You look like you could use some rest. Now, let me see how bad you are hurt. Take your coat off, and I'll get a good look at you.

In the dim light of the lantern, Tom looked into the old man's eyes. They had a kind, knowing look that spelled trust. Tom winced in pain as he struggled to take off the coat. Gerald carefully helped him. "Now, let's take a look at that bloody head." The older man scrutinized the wound. "Looks like you hit something real hard, like a rock. You're going to have a goose egg in the morn. What else hurts?"

"My side here." Tom pointed to the place.

"I'm gonna check and see if you got any broken ribs. Tell me if it hurts and how bad." The old man gently touched where Tom had shown and began to make ever-widening circles around the spot slowly. Tom winced in pain. The old man spoke, "The good news is, nothing's broken. The bad news is, you're gonna be sore for some time, but you'll survive."

Tom laughed, but it hurt. He winced in pain again. "What do I owe the good physician for his services?"

"There's no charge. Your account was paid in full a long time ago." His response puzzled Tom, but he said nothing to his kind host. "I have some jerky and bread, and we can have a spot of tea to wash it all down."

Quickly, the old man got two tin plates and a couple of chipped cups. He poured the hot water from the stove into the cups and dropped a tea bag in each. He got some dark brown jerky from another large glass jar, and then bread from a tin box. He placed these on the two plates for the men's supper. Another piece of jerky, he threw to the big cat that devoured it.

He then bowed his head and prayed, "Lord, bless this meager meal to our bodies. Help this young man to heal in his body and in ways he's not even aware of. Amen."

"Amen," Tom said. *Strange prayer from an odd but kind man.*

The men ate the meal with little talking. Tom was tired. "Got some canned peaches for dessert. Want some?" asked Gerald.

"Sure," said Tom. "This banquet just keeps getting better and better." Tom looked at Gerald, "I thank you for your kindness, but please, tell me who you are."

Gerald paused and smiled. "Like I told you, my name is Gerald, and I'm here to help you. If I was going to do you harm, don't you think I would have done it already?"

Tom nodded his head. "Yeah, I suppose so."

"Tomorrow, we'll talk. Give me that plate when you're done. Can't say bedding is much here. I always used a rolled-up bamboo mat like they do in the Orient. Got some army blankets to keep you warm, if the fire dies down. And, oh, Kitty may cuddle up next to you. She's nice and warm, but there's a tradeoff."

"Fleas?" asked Tom.

"No, she snores."

The two men finished eating, and Gerald washed the dishes and cup in a bucket. He showed Tom the mats and blankets and pointed to a spot on the dirt floor where he could sleep. The exhausted Tom was soon asleep on the mat. Gerald spoke as he looked at Tom. "Poor man could have slept on a sack of rocks as tired as he was. Lord, help me meet his needs and point him in the right direction tomorrow. Lord, please don't let me fail."

Chapter 14

Tom slowly rolled over on the mat that separated him from the floor. His side and head hurt, but he'd slept reasonably sound on the hard surface. His sleep had been free of the nightmares that sometimes caused him to awaken in a cold sweat since leaving Vietnam.

The smell of cooking food rolled across his nostrils, and it smelled good. He sat up and saw old Gerald fixing something in a skillet and a pot on the flat-topped iron heat stove.

"Well, my young friend, I trust you slept well. I hope you're feeling better this morning. I got some jerky heating and water for some grits and cowboy coffee. It's that Chock full O' Nuts brand. I like it because it's that heavenly coffee, you know. Hope that suits you," said Gerald.

Tom's stomach growled. "That sounds good to me. Thank you. And yes, I'm feelin' better this morning. My side and head still hurt, but it's tolerable. Like you said last night, healing will take a few days."

"Good to hear that. We got lots to talk about after breakfast. The only bathroom of sorts for those human needs is the outhouse just around the rocks in front. Follow the path, and you can't miss it. I'll take care of our breakfast. And Kitty is somewhere out there. You wouldn't want to frighten 'er," he said as he grinned.

"Thanks for the info on Kitty. No, I wouldn't want to surprise her. And I do need to take care of business. That rumble in my gut's more than hunger."

Tom rose slowly to his feet. That fall into the arroyo would take a while to recover from. He could feel hurts all over, but his head and side ached worse. Gerald handed him his coat. It was challenging to put it on with so much in pain, but he managed. Tom opened the rough wood door to the cabin and stepped out into the chilly morning air. The sun was just above a mountain ridge that formed the eastern horizon far away.

The way to the outhouse was easy to see, as Gerald said. Tom walked down the path and around the rocks where he found the little shack with its well-weathered boards. It reminded him of some he'd seen and used back in the hills of home. He went in, dropped his drawers to his knees, and sat down just in time. How anything that looked and smelled so good going in could come out so stinking and nasty, he did not know. It was a mystery.

The wooden seat was cold on his bare skin, but he quickly forgot about it as he looked out the outhouse door that faced the east. Never in his life had he seen such stark beauty. The early light from the sun danced on the rock formations that stretched as far as his eyes could see. It would be a horrible place to get lost, but he was overwhelmed with the colors in the rocks before him; muted yellows, deep reds, pinks, vermillion, and smoky whites in linear patterns. A picture indeed would be worth a thousand words, but even a million words couldn't do justice to all his eyes beheld. Tom sat for at least a minute absorbing the beauty in spite of the cold air. He forgot where he was until some passing gas reminded him why he was here. Nearby was an old Sears catalog, and Tom ripped a page from the book, the gun section, he noted. He tore out another page to finish off necessary paperwork and then pulled his pants and underwear over his cold bottom. *Strange.* His deposit down the hole seemed to be the only contribution lately. *Everything else at the bottom seems like it had been left there a long time ago.* He walked into the brilliant sunlight and again stopped to feast in nature's beauty. *Surely, this was done by a Master's hand.*

He walked hastily back to Gerald's old cabin. He opened the door and saw Kitty lying in the spot where she'd slept last night. The big cat raised her head to acknowledge Tom almost like a human would. Then she put her head on her paws in front of her and closed her eyes.

"About time you made it back. Thought you might have fell in, and I'd need to get a rope and pull you out," Gerald said.

"No, I'm fine. A little stiff, but everything came out okay. What I hadn't expected was to see such beauty here. Your outhouse must have the best view in the state, if not the whole country."

"I know," said Gerald. "Me and Kitty spent many a sunrise sitting on the rocks upwind from the outhouse basking in our Creator's morning performance. It never gets old. They call that area the Maze. Many an outlaw holed up there in years gone by. Butch Cassidy, the Sundance Kid, and Butch's gang, the Wild Bunch, had a place they called Robber's Roost out there. It has only one way in and one way out. A single man with a good rifle could hold off an army. Smart lawmen wouldn't go in there. Those that did never returned.

"Now, I got everything ready for you: coffee, grits with leftover peaches, some bread, and jerky bacon. I hope it meets your satisfaction. And I got some sugar and powdered milk for your coffee, if you like. Grab that stool and bring it over to my little table."

Tom said, "That meal sounds great. I like my coffee black. Is cowboy coffee like campfire coffee? I've had that."

"Yup, one and the same. Nothing like starting the day off with some strong coffee. But first, would you bless the meal?" asked Gerald.

Tom looked at him from across the small table and said, "I'm not used to praying, but I'll try to do my best. Lord, Creator of all things large and small, Creator of the great beauty I see here, bless this food to our bodies and give us strength today. Amen."

Gerald looked at Tom and said, "I thought you just said you weren't used to giving blessings. That prayer had all the marking of a preacher man. I've known clergy with lots of experience that couldn't give a sincere prayer like that. Now, no more time jawin'. Eat up." And they did.

The two hungry men gobbled the cowboy meal. They didn't talk and seemed to be studying each other. When they were done, Gerald took the dirty items and washed them in a bucket of water. He dried the plate and cups with a worn towel and then wiped his hands dry. "Now, let's get down to business," he said as he sat down. "I know why you're here. You're lost, more lost than you even know, and you're running from what you need to do." He let those words sink in. "And I'd like to try to help you."

"I don't think you can help me. I don't think anyone can."

"Try me. I have all day. I've got an eternity that I can wait, if necessary."

Tom looked at the older man, and somehow, he knew he wanted to trust Gerald. He'd befriended Tom when he really needed a friend and had asked nothing in return. Still, something held him back from opening up. "Why don't you tell me about yourself? What are you doing out here in the middle of nowhere, and how did you ever get a mountain lion named Kitty for a pet?"

Gerald smiled. "Guess I do owe you somewhat of an explanation. You know my name. I grew up in Green River and have family over there. Back in 1941, I got a call from Uncle Sam and ended up in the Marines fighting the Japanese across every God-forsaken, mosquito-infested island in the Pacific. I got sick a couple of times from who knows what diseases but always got better in spite of the medics and doctors. I never got shot somehow, but in the confusion of one battle, I ended up behind enemy lines and was captured. I weighed 96 pounds when our prison camp was liberated. I saw more horror and cruelty than a thousand men in a thousand lifetimes should see. The Japs knew they couldn't hold the position and were killing everyone to try to cover up their horrible deeds. They were shooting, bayoneting, and clubbing Americans and a few British prisoners in the prison camp to death. One hit me in the head with the butt of his gun. He thought he'd killed me and left me for dead. The blow that knocked me cold saved my life. The rest of those alive, they herded into a building and set it afire. Anyone who attempted to escape they shot.

"The next day, the Marines arrived. Out of 542 men, only ten survived. They found me more dead than alive. My head was split open, and Uncle Sam did the best he could to patch me up, but my fighting days were over. You see, the surgeons put a steel plate in my head to make up for the busted skull. They told me if I ever bumped it wrong, it could kill me. They gave me a medical discharge, GI benefits, and a war-related disability stipend that came once every month.

"When I got back home to Green River, I found I had no desire to be around people anymore. So I found this place, built this cabin, and here I lived happily ever after, more or less. Once a month, I go into town, pick up my check, and get the supplies I need."

Tom asked, "And what about the cat? How did you get Kitty?"

"I always had a way with animals. There was never a horse or dog, no matter how wild I couldn't tame. Cats are a whole different critter. I found Kitty all broke up and hurt. She looked like she'd been in a big fight and came out second best. When I first tried to help her, she took a swat at me and gave me this scar on my cheek. I guess she thought I was trying to harm her. I was more careful after that. To make a long story short, I nursed her back to health, but it did take quite a while, and when she got healthy and well enough to go, she wouldn't go, and that's how I got me a Kitty. Ain't that right, girl?"

The big cat, who'd been observing, puckered up her face and growled pleasantly.

"See," said Gerald. "She understands me."

Tom nodded his head in agreement. The man and cat did seem to be able to communicate despite their differences.

"Okay, young man. You've heard my story. Now, tell me yours. What are you doing out here in the middle of nowhere, as if I don't know?"

Tom was now ready to tell his tale. "I got in some trouble back home, and my choice was jail or the Army. I took the Army and ended up in Vietnam. There was a battle that lasted three days. I saw many men die horrible deaths. I had some friends; one died almost immediately, shot through the head. I still remember wiping his brains off my face. Somehow, me and Chris, a big Navajo Indian, managed to survive the hell till the last day. A Huey chopper came in carrying supplies that kept us in the fight and not overrun by the North Vietnamese Regulars. We unloaded the goods and were loading the helicopter with dead and wounded men. They were stacked like cordwood; there were so many. I took a round. Chris was in the process of throwing me in the chopper when he was hit in the chest with numerous rounds. I managed to pull him in, and the Huey took off. He was lying on top of me, eye-to-eye bleeding to death. His dying request was that I tell his dad that he died in battle, and I promised Chris I would. He lived on the big Navajo reservation in Arizona. I chickened out, and my stomach churns every time I think about it. I know I should go, but I can't bring myself to do it. I'm miles from where I should be. I can't do it. And on top of that, every time I hear an explosion, whether it's firecrackers or a truck backfiring, my mind tells me I'm back in Vietnam in battle."

Neither man spoke after Tom finished his tale. The big cat watched attentively but remained silent. After a long pause, Tom got up and said, "I think I need some air and some time to think."

Gerald nodded, "You take all the time you want. I ain't goin' nowhere. Got all the time in the world. I'll be here at the cabin, Kitty and me."

Tom went out and climbed up the red sandstone cliff until he was high above the cabin. The sun danced on rock formations that went on for what seemed forever. He found a suitable spot and sat. *What am I gonna do?*

Several hours passed as Tom pondered the question. He knew what he needed to do; there was no way around it.

He rose from the hard, cold sandstone and looked to the area called the Maze to the east. He could understand now why Gerald had chosen this hill for his home. Someday, he hoped he could return again during better times. Tom walked down to the cabin and entered. Gerald and the big cat acknowledged his presence, but he remained silent. Tom smelled soup warming on the stove and saw hot water for coffee heating.

"I'm gonna do it," said Tom.

"Gonna do what?" asked Gerald.

"I'm gonna keep the promise I made to Chris. I'm goin' to go see his dad."

Gerald's rawhide face lit up. "Well, praise be. I so hoped that would be the choice you made. I'd have a tough time looking myself in a mirror if I reneged on a promise. Chris's father really should know what happened from someone who was with Chris. I think it'll mean the world to him."

"I hope you're right. I think I'd almost want to face the gooks again than finish this task. It ain't gonna be easy telling him about his son's death."

"No, it won't, but it will help bring closure for his father."

Tom nodded his head. "Looks like my generous host has soup for lunch. Could we have some soon? I don't know how I can ever repay you for all you've done. I'd like to be goin' after lunch. I've got a long way to go," he paused, "if I knew how to get out of here."

"Did you see a big fireball explosion before you came here?"

"Why yes, how did you know?"

"The Army's been testing rockets that cruise. Top Secret Stuff, but everyone around here knows about it. They've been launching them from two pads just east of Green River, and they're supposed to land downrange at White Sands in New Mexico. Most, but not all, are doing just that. It seems the system has a few bugs that need worked out. With one, they tried to wake up the dead down in some little town in Mexico. It landed in a cemetery and made the locals mad till Uncle Sam fixed up the graveyard better than new and greased some of the state officials' palms. All the hoopla died down soo after that. Another rocket didn't stop and kept going. It's probably in the waters of the Pacific Ocean, or maybe the Amazon jungles of Brazil. No one knows. And one crashed and burned yesterday 'bout a mile away from here a couple of hills over. Then, you showed up."

"My vehicle's over there if there's anything left of it. Can you take me back so I can see what I'm gonna have to do?"

"Sure, you'll never find it if I don't show you. I want you to remember the trail. You may want to come back sometime. You'd be welcomed."

Tom nodded his approval, and they placed the food on the table to eat. After a short prayer, the two men chowed down on the meager meal. Shortly after they finished, Gerald told Tom it was time to go. They left the dishes on the rustic table, and with the big cat in the lead, headed out the door. The ground was still frozen. Tom said he worried that if it thawed and turned to mud, he may not be able to drive out, that is if his microbus was still in one piece.

They walked for about a half-hour down a trail little more than a trace. Tom observed the path they traveled carefully. Someday, he may return, and Gerald was right. He'd never found his way out on his own, but he was reasonably sure he could find his way back again.

They came around a blind bend, and in the distance, Tom saw his VW. It looked intact, and there were men, trucks, and heavy equipment all busy at work nearby. There'd been no conversation between the men as they walked, and the big cat had also been strangely quiet.

Gerald spoke. "This is as far as me and Kitty go. You don't need us anymore. Our job's done."

"Thank you ever so kindly for your help. I'd still be cold, hungry, lost, and maybe dead if it wasn't for you."

"Glad I could help you, young man. Often in life, you'll find helpers arrive and often from the most unlikely places when you need it. Never forget that."

Tom turned and gave the old, gnarly man a big hug. "Thanks again. You're a lifesaver."

Gerald was embarrassed but did his best to return the embrace. "Well, I guess this is goodbye."

"Yeah," said Gerald. "I guess it is. I never was very good at saying goodbye. I have a favor to ask of you. I have a message for my brother Ray. My brother is a great guy. You can depend on him. He runs Ray's Pub over in Green River. It's a great place for a brew and a burger. He cuts his own potatoes for French fries, too. Would you tell him, 'I'm okay where I am, and thanks for all he's done for me. I miss him, and Dad misses him too.' Promise you'll do that for me."

"I will. I promise. You've helped me see the importance of keeping your promise."

"You better get goin'. You can make it to Green River and have supper at Ray's. It shouldn't be too busy this time of year. He gets a bunch of cruisers and tourists in the summertime."

"I'll miss you, my friend."

"And I, you."

Tom walked off. At a short distance, he turned and said, "I hope to see you again." Gerald said nothing, but raised his hand and waved goodbye. The big cat sat next to Gerald with his tail wrapped around him. Tom waved back, turned to go, and as he turned, he thought he heard Gerald say, “I don’t think we can.”

Tom didn’t turn back but walked on toward the distant microbus. Gerald watched Tom get ever smaller in the distance. He put his hand on the cat’s big head and scratched behind her ears. She liked it and rubbed her face on his leg. “Well, Kitty, we’ve done what we can. The rest is up to him.”

***

Tom walked up to the busy to-do. An armed man stopped him and took him to another man who questioned him about what business he had being here. Tom told him he’d been at an old cabin in the hills, this was his vehicle, and he was going to Green River. That satisfied the man who seemed to be in charge of this beehive of activity. He told Tom to forget everything he saw. Tom knew that meant the ruined rocket on the back of a flatbed. Workers were covering it up with a large tarp. Tom said he understood, and his lips were sealed. He’d recently left the Army, and he knew the importance of secrecy.

Tom looked at his vehicle covered with dust, but other than that, it was like he had left it. It growled a few times as he cranked the cold engine but finally started. He wove his way through the heavy equipment and trucks. The area ahead was scorched black. It had to be where the rocket crashed and exploded. The vegetation, not burned up, was charred. Tom passed this scene of destruction quickly and traveled up the frozen road. At the hard-topped highway, he saw the Canyonlands sign that had sidetracked him on his adventure.

He looked both ways, turned right back onto Utah Route 24, and saw a sign, “Green River, 40 miles”. *Ray’s Pub shouldn’t be hard to find in a small town. Bet Ray will be surprised when he gets the message Gerald gave me.*

Chapter 15

The hour drive into Green River went quickly. The road was good except for the last section near the small town. Tom had been in the middle of nowhere and still was, but there was a sign that read, "Interstate 70, scheduled date of completion, 1968. Your tax dollars at work."

There was next to no traffic on the state highway, and the streets in the town had even less. Why anyone would put a four-lane road here was a mystery to the young man. *Wonder what Great White Father in Washington came up with this boondoggle? Someone must have pulled some strings.*

Tom rode by some motels and gas stations. One was the Robber's Roost Motel. The big chain motels hadn't arrived in the oasis of Green River yet. He stopped at the only traffic light in town on a red and waited. His was the single vehicle he saw moving in the whole community presently. An old whitewashed church with a tall steeple stood proudly on his left, and it had a cemetery next to it. *Bet there're way more people in the town cemetery than living here today*. An empty two-story red brick building was at the corner just passed the light, and it had two large colorful signs painted on the street side. One read, Green River Grocery, and the other under it read, Ray's Pub, Best Grub in Town. A large red arrow separated them and pointing the way to the two stores.

Tom turned his signal on, though there was no one on the street who needed to know of his intentions. The light changed to yellow, then green, and he turned the VW hippie microbus down First Street. He passed Ray's Pub on the left and continued to the grocery store. It was a nondescript block building with an ice machine out front, but he doubted many people were buying ice. The small store was a surprise. For a place that had to be near the end-of-the-earth, it had a good selection and quantity of goods and groceries, and the check-out staff was friendly. Tom commented to them about his pleasant surprise on the many items of good quality in their story. The cashier laughed and said that this was the only place in miles, and everyone came here or did without.

Tom walked out of the door with his supplies, and a cop stood between him and his van looking at it.

The cop who looked like he was in his 50s asked matter-of-fact-like, “This your van?”

“Yes, it is, officer. Is there a problem?”

“Got any drugs on ya?”

Not again. “No, sir. No drugs. Nothin’. I just got out of the Army, bought this thing from some hippies in San Francisco, got searched in Zion by two park rangers with a dog named Deputy Dawg. The canine found one damned seed the previous owners had left. I thought I was getting busted, but they let me go.”

“Deputy Dawg, you say? That shepherd has the best nose in the west.” He paused for effect. “So, you just got out of the Army? Where did you serve?”

“Vietnam, got shot, the Army discharged me for medical, and I’m now on my way back home to West Virginia.”

“Thanks for serving. I was in WWII.” Then, he said, “You may want to think about getting that van repainted. It draws all kinds of attention you don’t want or need.”

"Yeah, I've wanted to do that. Just don't have the money for anything but a gallon of house paint, and I don't want to ruin the van."

"You do what you can. It'll make your life easier with the men in blue. That paint job is a cop magnet." The radio in the patrol car went off. Tom could hear the dispatcher calling for the officer. He got out his portable radio at his hip and spoke into it, "This is Harold. What's up Trudy?"

"Harold, we got a 10-90 at 112 Anderson Street."

"Roger that. I'm on my way."

"10-90?" asked Tom.

"Domestic violence. Old man Smith must be drunk again and taking his frustrations out on his old lady. This ain't gonna be pretty. I told him if he hit her again, somebody was gonna get an ass whippin'. He got it comin', and it will do more good than locking him up. Got to go, kid. Good luck on your travels."

"One question before you go. How is the food at Ray's?"

"It's great, the best in town, and I'd say that even if he wasn't my brother. Like I said, I got to go. Someone needs an attitude adjustment," and with that, he jumped into the patrol car and was gone.

Tom placed the groceries in the back of the microbus to use later. A huge greasy hamburger smothered in onions, pickle relish, and ketchup, Heinz, he hoped, along with some fresh-cut French fries and a cold beer would be a thing of beauty for his stomach. He made a U-turn in the broad street and headed the short distance back to Ray's Pub. There was a dirt parking lot next to the establishment for customers. It was empty, and Tom was pretty sure he'd be their first customer. A buxom waitress was unlocking the door. "Come on in," she said. "Pick a spot, any spot. The big lunch crowd hasn't arrived yet, and probably won't till some warm weather arrives."

"Okay, I'll do that." He found a booth with thick padding and took a seat. She handed him a menu. "No need for that. I know what I want. Give me a big ole burger with lots of onions, pickle relish, and ketchup on it, and a large order of fries. I've been Ray's has the best burgers in town."

"As small as our town is, that ain't saying much," she said, smiling, "but this I guarantee, you won't be disappointed. No, sir. They're a treat for your tongue and gullet."

"That sounds great. And your best lager beer to wash it all down," he said. "And could I have a word with the owner afterward? Someone asked me to pass a message on to him."

"I'll take your order to Ray. He's in the kitchen. I'll tell him you want to talk to him, but it won't be until after you're done with your meal. I hope that's okay."

Tom said it was. She went in the back and spoke to someone. He could hear a male voice answering. She came out, grabbed a beer mug, and filled the clear glass with the golden liquid. The waitress brought it over to Tom and sat it down. "Here you go. The best burger and fries in the Beehive State of Utah will be out shortly. Ray said he could talk after the meal. He's getting things ready for lunch."

"Okay, now let me taste that beer." He took the mug to his lips and sipped. It was good, very good. He nodded his approval and gave a thumbs up to the waitress.

"That's a great local beer, Green River Lager. We ain't all tea toting Mormons in Utah. And if you think that was tasty, wait till you bite into the burger and fries," she said.

She left Tom with his beer, which he happily sipped. He looked around the pub. It had lots of exposed wood timbers, a long bar with stools on one wall, a pool table in the back, and T-shirts pinned to the walls from what must have been every whitewater rafting outfit in the area. *Wonder how that got there?* Tom stared at one that read, Youghiogheny River Runners, Ohiopyle, Pennsylvania. That was close to home. It reminded him he needed to call his dad and see how he was doing with the Parkinson's.

She soon reappeared with a tray carrying the biggest burger and a plate of fries Tom had ever seen. He finished off the mug and ordered another. Hungry Tom jumped right into the food. Grease dripped down his face from his satisfied mouth. *Oh, I've died and gone to heaven.* The home cut fries watered in his mouth. *Oh, this is good.* The waitress brought another mug of beer Tom would need to wash the belly-buster of a meal down. A man appeared behind the bar that he assumed was Ray. The man looked at Tom and asked, "You the guy that wants to see me?" Tom had his mouth full of food, so he smiled and nodded. "I have a few things to do in the back. So, how about I catch you when you've finished off the meal?" Tom nodded in agreement. Ray disappeared into the back while Tom ate his meal. A few minutes later, Ray walked to the table and asked the very satisfied and stuffed Tom, "Now, what was it you needed to see me about? Sammy said you had a message for me."

"First off, let me say the burger and fries were great, and your waitress picked a good beer, too. You've got a super place, and if I ever get back this way, I'll make a point of stopping in."

"Thanks for the compliment. We may be about the only place in town, but we have always tried to be the best in a hundred miles or better." He paused, "So, you have a message from my brother. What does he have to say? Did Harold give you a ticket?"

"No, he didn't give me a ticket though I did just meet him when I drove into town."

"Oh, then it must have been my brother Darold. He runs the general store and fillin' station down in Hanksville. I bet you got a bite to eat there and gassed up the tank, too."

"Well, yeah, I did do that, but I didn't know he was your brother. The message is from your other brother, Gerald. I met him out in Canyonlands. He said to tell you he's okay where he is. Thanks for all you've done for him, and he and Dad were fine, and they miss you."

The smile disappeared from Ray's face. He shifted uneasily in his seat. His elbows came to rest on the table, and he looked sharply into Tom's eyes. He asked, "What did this man look like?"

Now it was Tom's turn to be uneasy. "He a… he a… he looked a lot like you, a little shorter and thinner. He was missing some front teeth, and he had a big scar on his cheek."

"Which cheek?"

"The left one," Tom said. "And it ran up and down from his eye almost to his chin. And another thing, he had a pet mountain lion, a female, he called Kitty."

Ray sat back in his chair. "Young man, that sure sounds like my brother, Gerald. That's what he looked like. And he did have a pet mountain lion, but Gerald's been dead a year. He's buried less than a quarter-mile from here in the churchyard you passed on the way."

Neither man said anything for a moment. Tom was too shocked to speak. Ray continued, "He'd come into town around the first of every month from his shack out by Canyonlands and pick up his military disability check and buy some supplies. I'd drive him back out as far as we could go. Last December, the weather was bad, awful, so when he didn't show up, we didn't think much about it. It stayed nasty for about a week and then improved. He still was a no-show. Harold and me went out looking for him. We found his cabin up in the rocks. That big cat was guarding the place. It took her a while to decide we were friendly. I guess she saw the family resemblance, and she finally let us go in. We found Gerald on his mat frozen. The animals would have got to his body if not for that big cat."

"We brought his body into town, and the coroner did an autopsy. He said there was no sign of foul play, and he likely died in his sleep. The death certificate listed 'natural causes' as what done him in. We should all be so lucky to die in our sleep."

At last, Tom found his voice. "Mister, I know this sounds strange and beyond belief, but if not for your brother, I'd probably died out there in that rocky place. I didn't come in here seeking to cause trouble, only to deliver his message."

Ray was silent now. He sighed deeply and spoke, "The man you described sure sounds like my brother. He was always helping people that got lost out there in that maze of rocks. It looks like his spirit still is."

"Hey Sammy, do you think you can run this place without me today? "

"I can. I'll manage without you. You know it's been really slow."

"Good. I've got some things I want to show this young man." Then he looked at Tom and said, "I think we need to pay our respects at the graveyard and then go out to his old cabin in Canyonlands. I think we should. How about you, young man?"

"I think you are right. You're not the only one with unanswered questions."

***

The grave was just as Ray said it was at the churchyard. A small wooden cross with the name Gerald Arnone and the date of death were carved on it. They rode in silence the hour out to Canyonlands. Tom led the way up to the old cabin. It looked like no one had been there for a year, but they noted fresh mountain lion tracks in the sandy-mud mix nearby. They found the old outhouse with the best view in America, and someone had used it recently. Neither said much on the hike out or the ride back to Green River. It was getting dark when they got back to Ray's Pub.

Sammy fixed up two hot steak sandwiches, onion rings, and beers for the men. They said little as they ate. Each was deep in his thoughts. They finished their meals at about the same time. Ray smiled and spoke, "Looks like we have a real mystery here. I still don't know what to make of your story, but I don't take you to be a malicious type of person. When you work with the public, you learn quick to size up a person, and I've had a lot of practice."

Tom said, "I assure you, I meant no harm. I'm kinda confused about this whole matter myself, and I owe you for two great meals. We were in such a big hurry when we left; I didn't pay. What do I owe you?"

"What do you own me? Nothing. You had me thinking about the good old times us four boys had growin' up together, and that was worth far more than two meals."

Tom got up. "I want to thank you, too for what you've done." He walked toward the front door.

"Hey, young man," he heard Ray say. "What's your name?"

Tom grimaced. He'd been with this man all day and not told him his name. "Why it's Tom, Tom Kenney."

"I have a favor to ask you, Mister Kenney."

"Sure, whatever you want."

"If you ever see my brother again, tell him we miss him and Dad deeply, and we're doin' okay, too."

Tom said he would and left the building. He stopped at the Green River KOA Kampgound for the night. The muddy waters of the fast-flowing stream going over some large rocks would lull him to sleep that night. *What had happened today, and what did it mean?* He didn't know, but tomorrow he knew he'd head for the Navajo Nation where Chris Benally's father lived. *What surprises were in store for him there?* He would have to play this hand out and see.

Chapter 16

Tom woke at sunrise. The morning in the high desert was cold but clear, and the night wind that buffeted the microbus and rocked him to sleep had subsided. He made a quick trip to the warm bathhouse at the RV park. Tom fixed a quick breakfast with the supplies he had purchased the day before and was soon underway east on the highway toward Moab. As he drove, he thought of the events of yesterday. He was still unsure of what to make of the happenings. Given time, he hoped he would make some sense of it all.

One hour later, he pulled up to the entrance booth at Arches National Park. He paid the admission fee and drove up the twisting road into the park. For the next hour, he did a stop, look, and go at the many large stone arches in the park. The little brochure said that this area contained over two thousand of them. It had a higher concentration of the stone horseshoe like structures than any other place on earth, and his eyes told him to believe it. No two were alike. Some were single; some were joined. One group was three arches end to end. Some were delicate, and others were massive.

He drove on to a lot leading to the arch pictured on the front of the handout. It took a two-mile walk to get to the arch's location, but it only a one-half mile hike for a good view still from a distance. Tom only had enough time for the latter. Today was going to be a long day, and he was not sure he would make Lukachukai by nightfall, but with the camper, he could stop whenever he got tired. Tom walked up the path past some petroglyphs and saw a sign that read John Wesley Wolf Cabin, Two Hundred Feet. An arrow pointed the way. Tom wondered what kind of a man would try to make a life in this barren, but beautiful land. The trail turned and twisted along a calm, but murky stream of water. He rounded a corner and stopped dead in his tracks. His eyes fell on the small old cabin, and his mouth dropped open, and he gasped. The old cabin looked just like Gerald's in Canyonlands. Tom slowly walked forward to the small structure. The door was locked, so he looked into the window. The interior looked just like he remembered Gerald's cabin. He began to shake. *No. This can't be. What's happening to me?*

He sat down on a park bench nearby to catch his breath. It took a while to regained his composure. He wasn't sure what was going on, but he knew he needed to leave this place and keep moving. Traveling down the highway would give him time to think.

Tom walked quickly to his vehicle, hopped in, and drove out of the park. He'd seen enough. The small town of Moab disappeared in his rearview mirror as he rode south on US 191. A sign announced the large arch to his left off the highway as Wilsons Arch. He saw the two signs several miles apart that pointed to Canyonlands, but he'd seen enough of that place for his liking. "I've had enough adventures for a while," he said, his thought rolling out his mouth. "Hope I can make it there before nightfall."

Another sign ten miles down the road announced a massive rock outcropping in a field as Church Rock. He could see a hole big enough to drive a dump truck in at the base. *Guess they must have used that cavern as a church in olden days. Wonder what the acoustics were like when the singing started?*

The road was in good condition and straight. Even in the under-powered VW, Tom was making good time. A few long, steep grades slowed him down, but these weren't many. He passed a tall twin rock that looked like great hands had sculptured it, and it was right behind a large restaurant. *If that thing ever falls, the restaurant is history. I wouldn't want to be anywhere near if that happens.*

At the town of Bluff, he turned on US 163, a very scenic route that crossed the San Juan River. It was the largest stream he'd seen since Green River. Within a few miles, he saw another sign, Welcome to Monument Valley, Navajo Nation. It was self-evident why John Ford and John Wayne made so many movies in this area. The rocks, everything about this area, just shouted that you were in the Wild West. As he drove down the slight incline toward the massive rock formations ahead known as the Mittens, he thought he saw a blue box about the size of a phone booth along the side of the road, and then a bearded man with a headband running and a group of people following him ran by. *Is this real?* He kept driving, and they never acknowledged that they saw Tom. A quarter-mile down the road, he looked in the rearview mirror, but there was nothing there, no people, and no blue box.

At the little town of Kayenta, he realized he'd taken a wrong turn and needed to get back on US 191. "Too many distractions," he muttered. This long cut would cost him an extra hour of travel. He found US 191 again, turned right, and traveled for another 45 minutes till he saw a speed sign for the little town of Round Rock. The notice was almost bigger than the town. If he'd blinked his eyes, he'd have missed it and another sign that pointed to the left and said, Lukachukai, 16 miles.

A short time later, he pulled the hippie microbus into Likachukai. It wasn't much to look at, some trailers that had seen better days and many nondescript prefab homes that looked like they had all been cut with the same cookie cutter. He passed Totsoh Trading Post, the community's general store. The Chapter House had to be around here somewhere. Tom knew from talking with Chris while in Vietnam, this was the place to go to find the house of

Dark Cloud Benally. It served as the Indian town hall and information center all rolled into one.

He pulled into the parking lot in front of the building and slid to a stop on a skiff of ice and snow. The wind tore at his coat as he got out of the brightly painted microbus. Brown faces appeared at the windows and stared out at his vehicle. Suspicion was written all over their faces. *Yup, they're expecting another unwelcome drugged-out hippie looking for peyote, I bet. Can't say I blame them. I got to get some new paint on this van.*

He went into the warm building and looked around. About ten pairs of dark eyes looked at him warily, Tom didn't like the looks of this, and he felt very self-conscious. He cleared his throat and said, "A friend of mine told me if I needed to find someone here on the Big Rez, the Chapter House was the place to start. Could anyone please tell me where Dark Cloud Benally lives?"

From Tom's right, a man's voice spoke, "Who wants to know and why?"

Tom couldn't see who had spoken. Four men and a woman sat in that direction, and all had long braided hair and leathery faces. "My name is Tom Kenney. I came a long way to deliver a message to him. I was with his son Chris in Vietnam."

Tom could see dark eyes widening as his statement sank in. The oldest-looking of the men spoke, "Hosteen Benally is in the back room. He's busy helping someone with a problem. Wait here till he's done. Then you can see him."

"Thank you." He sat down next to a fat and very pregnant Navajo girl. "Hello," he said to be polite.

"Ya`at`eeh," she replied. Tom looked puzzled. She smiled. "I said, hello.'"

"And a ya`at`eeh to you, too." He smiled politely and looked around the room. The people had gone back to their business. Some were playing cards and checkers. Two played a game he did not know. Occasionally, they looked in his direction, but none seemed too concerned about the strange white boy who'd somehow found his way to this remote corner of the Big Reservation.

About ten minutes passed slowly for Tom. A door opened in the back of the building, and two people, an older man and a younger man, emerged. They were still talking, but Tom couldn't make out what they were saying in Navajo. As they spoke, the man who'd questioned Tom walked to them and whispered into the older man's ear. He seemed surprised and unsure as his eyes met Tom's. He said something more to the young man who walked to the front of the building and exited. The older man then came to Tom, who rose. He had his hand out, which Tom shook. "Hello. I'm Dark Cloud Benally. I understand you want to speak with me."

Tom nodded. "I think it would be best if we spoke in private. What I have to say is of a very personal matter."

Dark Cloud said, "Okay," and led him to a table in the back of the room. Tom figured the man was uncertain as to Tom's intentions and didn't trust him, or they would have gone to the back room and closed the door. Why should he?. If Tom were in his shoes or moccasins, he wouldn't trust him if the situation was reversed.

They took seats at the table at the back of the room. Tom knew every person in the place was watching him but tried to ignore it. "So," Dark Cloud said, " I hear you come along ways to deliver me a message. It must be very important. Would you please tell me what it is?"

.

Chapter 17

Tom nodded. "I think it would be best if we spoke in private. What I have to say is of a very personal matter."

Dark Cloud said, "Okay," and led him to a table in the back of the room. Tom figured the man was uncertain as to Tom's intentions and did not trust him, or they would have gone to the back room and closed the door. Tom could not blame the man. If he were in his shoes or moccasins, he wouldn't trust him if the situation was reversed.

They took seats at a table in the back of the room. Tom could tell that every person in the room was watching him, but trying to be discreet about it. "So I hear you come a long way to deliver me a message. As I said before, it must be very important. What it is?" asked Dark Cloud. "You served with my son, and you were with him when he died, you said?"

Tom nodded his head. "We were friends, and yes, I was with him when he died. He asked me to give you a message. He said…"

"Stop. I want to hear the whole story. I need to know it all. I can cancel most of the appointments I have this afternoon and rearrange them for later, except for the one lady I see waiting. I'll take her and be free in about half an hour. Then we can talk. Is that good?"

"Okay," said Tom. "I think that would be better."

"There's not much to see or do in Lukachukai, but you could walk over to the Trading Post and look around till I get done."

"Okay, I'll do that and see you in a half-hour."

Dark Cloud said, "Better make it a little longer. You're on Indian time here."

"What does that mean?"

"It means it's kind of flexible. Could be up to an hour."

"Okay," said Tom. "There's no hurry. That will be all right."

"Yes. Now you are starting to think like an Indian."

Tom opened his mouth to speak about being part Indian but closed it. It could wait. "See you then. Bye."

"Ah koo' neh koo'. Goodbye, and see you back here soon."

Tom nodded, rose, and left. He felt all eyes in the room following him, and they were overflowing with questions. As he opened the chapter house door, cold wind hit his face and tried to tear the door handle from his hand, but he managed to hold on and forced it shut behind him. The gust tore at his jacket as he walked across the frozen dirt parking lot to the trading post with two old gas pumps. From what he'd seen of the area, filling stations were few and far between. He made a mental note to fill up here and not take any chances. Running out of gas wasn't in this desolate area would be bad.

He opened the trading post door and entered. The warm air on his face felt so good after having the frigid air tearing at his face. The five or six brown faces in the store turned at the stranger and quickly went back to their shopping. Tom walked around the store that seemed like a cross between a convenience store with the usual snack foods and soft drinks, a bulk store, and Navajo gift store. Large cloth bags containing items such as flour and sugar sat next to large cans of what he assumed held lard. Fortunately, most things had English labels, besides Navajo, but one little area off to the side had only the Navajo items. It had beautiful woven blankets and rugs plus locally crafted grass baskets along with other handcrafted items like knives, kid's toys, and things only the occasional lost tourist who stumbled this desolate place would buy. *It may not be the end of the world, but you can see it from here.*

"Can I help you find something, young man?" came a voice behind him.

Tom turned and saw a man old enough to be his father. "I was just looking around. I got some time to kill." Tom realized he and the other man were the only two left in the store. Somehow and for some reason, the others had left. "How's business?"

"Not so good this time of the month. Government checks come around the first." He paused and looked at Tom. "What brings you to this area? We don't get too many tourists this time of year."

"In all honesty, sir, I was planning on skipping coming here and being in Colorado now, but you might say the spirit moved me to come here."

The man's eyes widened." I hope they were friendly spirits. There seems to be a lot of chindi roaming lately."

"Chindi? What are chindi?" asked Tom

"You must not be from around here. Chindi are spirits and leave the body with a person's last breath. They are everything bad about a person that can't go to the place of harmony. They can make people ill, and some even die from the sickness they cause."

Tom was a little surprised. "Sure sounds like something I want no part of. I think I'll get a Nehi and some chips and sit over by the wood stove for a while. It's awful nasty outside. Is it always like this, cold and windy?"

"It just turned cold today. It can get bitter cold in this valley, and it seems like it's always windy."

Tom got the soft drink and chips and paid the storekeeper. "This should do it," and he handed the man two dollars.

"Yes, it will. Here's your change," and he held the coins out to Tom, who took them. "What's your business on the Big Rez, young man?"

Tom said, "I'm here to see a man, Dark Cloud Bennally. I have something for him."

"Hosteen Dark Cloud? I hope you got some good news for him. He took it pretty hard when his son died in Vietnam."

Tom grimaced and took a drink of orange soda. "That's what I need to see him about. I was with his son when he died."

The storekeeper looked surprised, and nervously turned away. He was trying to hide behind a display of Slim Jims and pickled eggs. Seeing the conversation was over, Tom took a seat by the woodstove and nibbled at his purchases.

Several other people came into the store, made quick purchases, and left. The storekeeper made no more effort to talk with Tom and went back to his hiding place.

Tom wasn't sure what had happened. Maybe he'd committed a Navajo faux pas. He finished the Nehi and the potato chips. Still hungry, he purchased two Tillamook brand pickled sausages from the clerk who said little. Tom went back to the chair by the woodstove, sat down, and slowly ate the two sausages. There was no need to hurry. He was on Indian time.

A look at his watch told him it had been about 45 minutes, and Tom could see no reason to remain here. He finished the last of the sausage, got up, and walked out the door. The cold wind hit him again. *Man, I think the temperature's dropped ten degrees while I was here.*

Tom walked across the frozen parking area of the trading post. The asphalt road lacked a centerline, marking of any kind, and traffic, but he looked just the same. He continued to the chapter house avoiding an ice-filled pothole in the parking lot. The door handle was cold against Tom's bare hand as he turned it and entered. A comforting blast of hot air from an overhead heater welcomed him. Fewer people waited in the building, but again, all eyes turned to him but quickly looked away. *It seems like my novelty's already wearing off.*

He sat in an old overstuffed uncomfortable chair with broken springs. Dark Cloud was still busy in his office, so Tom picked up some magazines and papers from the book rack next to him. He glanced at his choices, most of them years old, and laid all back except for the newspaper, *The Navajo Times*. The front page looked pretty standard like any newspaper in America. "Sergeant Jim Chee and Lieutenant Joe Leaphorn arrested a suspect for the murder of a local man, Ben Cruz, whose corpse was found on Shiprock. Navajo Policeman Chee said over the course of a four-month investigation, he'd discovered evidence sufficient to lead to an arrest. Bernie Hillary of Farmington was apprehended at the Royale Inn. Officer Chee said items found at the scene led them to Hillary. The motive for the murder Chee said was a three-way love triangle gone bad. Hillary confessed to killing Cruz and also the third member of the triangle, Nancy Feinstein. Hillary said he dumped her body in the San Juan River near Mexican Hat, Utah. An extensive search of the river failed to find the body."

Tom's ears perked up. A conversation flowed from Dark Cloud Benally's office, but couldn't understand the Navajo spoken. A young woman exited the room and didn't seem happy. Dark Cloud appeared and motioned for Tom to come in. He placed the newspaper back in the rack and entered the office room. Dark Cloud said, "Take a seat," and he did.

"So, young man, you say you served with my son."

Tom said, "Yes, I did. I first met him at the army base in Georgia. We went through air infantry training there and then got shipped off to Vietnam."

Dark Cloud said, "During WWII, I served in the Pacific Theatre. The lady who just left before you, well, her father served there too. We were part of the Code Talkers, who provided secure and accurate information over the radios. She wanted me to see if I could get more disability benefits for her Dad. He got shot in the leg, and it never did heal right. I told her I would do what I could, but from the papers she showed me, I think he's already getting the maximum. I'm goin' give it a shot, but I told her the chances for success weren't good."

Tom said, "I've heard rumors about Code Talkers while in the Army. So, they really did exist?"

"Yes, some people know about it, but is still supposed to be secret," replied Dark Cloud. "The military will deny it ever happened. We weren't the first. They used some of the eastern tribes like the Choctaw and Cherokee for Code Talkers during WWI. The Navajos did secret communications in the Pacific Theatre, but Comanches, Meskwakis from Iowa, and even some Basque speakers contributed to the war effort in Europe and Africa."

"My dad served in Europe under Patton," said Tom. "He helped liberate some of the death camps. My dad's a very strong man. He's not a fellow to tear up easily, but whenever news on the TV has anything on the Holocaust, or the work camps comes on, he has to leave the room. I followed him one time. He didn't know I was there, but I could hear him sobbing. I left before he turned around and caught me."

Dark Cloud said, "War is hell. Any man who's been in battle has seen things no man should ever have to see."

Tom nodded his head in agreement. "Although I was only in Vietnam a short time, I saw things I never want to see again. Some things, I can't get it out of my mind. Sometimes I'll wake in a cold sweat with images of the men I saw die and some of them; I know I killed." Tom let out a deep sigh and placed his head in his hands. Dark Cloud said nothing as he watched the young man's behavior. Tom let out another sigh, put his hands down and raised his head. He looked at Dark Cloud and spoke, "War's hell."

Dark Cloud nodded his head knowingly and studied the young man in front of him. "Where are you staying tonight?"

"I've got a VW microbus that's set up for a camper. I bought it from some hippies in San Francisco, guess I didn't have to tell you that 'cause of the psychedelic paint job. That's the way it came."

Dark Cloud said with a smile, "You do stand out here on the Big Rez."

"That's an understatement if I ever heard one. That damn bus got me in trouble down in Utah. A couple of park rangers thought I was a doper, not a guy who'd just got out of the military. I gotta get me a new paint job before it leads to more troubles."

Dark Cloud nodded again. "I 'd like you to stay at my home tonight. It's not much, but it's better than freezing in the van."

"I really couldn't do that. I hardly know you, and I wouldn't want to impose on you.".

"I insist. You shall stay at my house tonight, and we'll have a fine supper. Sarah, my daughter, will have something delicious fixed, and then tomorrow at dawn, we'll visit my son's grave in the cemetery by the church."

Tom said, "Well if you put it like that, I accept."

"Good. Now let's get to know each other a little better, but don't tell me about the battle when my son died. Tell me about that tonight after supper."

The two men talked, sharing stories of their lives for the next hour and found they had much in common. They both enjoyed the time together, but Tom kept quiet about his Indian blood. That could wait for later. He had his reasons.

Dark Cloud glanced at his watch. A look of surprise came to his face. "I can't believe we've talked for over an hour. There's something I want to show you, and then we'll go to my house and have dinner."

"Okay, sounds like a plan," said Tom. "What do you want to show me?"

"Patience, young man. Patience. When you see it, you should understand."

They got up, left the room, and Dark Cloud locked the door behind him. He said, "In the good old days, we didn't need to do this. It's a shame that you can't even trust some members of your own tribe ."

Tom said nothing, and the two men exited the Charter House. The cold wind tore at the coats of the two men as they ran to the VW van and got in. *Just what was it Dark Cloud wanted to show him? What could be so important?*

Chapter 18

"Turn right at the road," Dark Cloud said.

Tom turned on a road that wound up the red rock canyon. A gigantic red stone monolith guarded the canyon on the left side of the colorful valley. Dark Cloud noted Tom's gaze at the cloven, split rock. "That's Butt Rock you're looking at. Some Indians say it's a brave showing his backside to the white man."

Tom laughed.

Dark Cloud continued, "I can see the resemblance, but I've always thought it looked more like a goat or sheep's hoof. Whatever it is, it's said to be the guardian of Lukachukai and this valley."

Tom nodded. "Where are we going? The sign we just passed said the road's closed from December to March, and it's early December."

"Got something I want to show you before the sun goes down." Usually, this road's closed during the winter because of snowfall, but this year's been very dry, and we've had next to no snow. We'll need the snow for water next year. The road's the responsibility of the reservation, and the tribe closes it up for liability purposes. Don't need nobody suing when they get stuck or run off the road. We don't have much snow removal equipment here, and it would be an unending job trying to keep it open. We don't have that kind of money. But as long as the snow don't fall, people can use it at their own risk, of course."

"Of course," said Tom. "I understand."

Dark Cloud laughed, "You needn't worry about me leading you into trouble. Remember this; I plan on having supper with you at my house tonight. Sarah should have mutton stew, fry bread, and coffee waiting for us when we get back."

"Thanks for the reassurance," said Tom. "Lunch was snacks from the trading post, and the ole stomach is telling me it's running on empty."

"Thought I heard your belly growling."

Tom nodded, and they continued up the beautiful canyon. Ponderosa pines growing on its slopes, replaced the junipers. They rounded a hairpin turn and then another almost as sharp, on the road now lightly covered with snow.

Dark Cloud looked over at Tom, "You do have good tires and know how to drive in snow, don't you?"

He met Dark Cloud's questioning eyes. "Yeah, I wouldn't have bought this thing if it had may-pops on it. And yes, I've driven in lots of snow in West Virginia."

"Good. You may need it soon. There's an area ahead where it likes to drift. Glad to hear you got no may-pops. Half the cars on the Big Rez have those," and he shook his head.

Tom saw the drift area, about a foot-and-a-half deep in places, but other vehicles had broken a path through it previously. Tom plowed into it, and the van's wheels slipped in the snow, tried to fishtail, but Tom corrected and got through the drift area. "Good driving," said Dark Cloud. "We're almost there. Turn at that gate on the right."

Tom did. Dark Cloud got out and opened the gate after using a key on the lock. He motioned Tom through. After he passed, Dark

Cloud closed the gate, locked it, walked to the van, and got in. "Just a little further."

Tom drove in a forest of tall ponderosa pines about a quarter of a mile.

"Stop here," said Dark Cloud. He got out as did Tom. "Follow me."

Dark Cloud led the way up a steep and winding path to the top of a cliff. "This is what I wanted to show you." He pointed off to the east. Tom saw a massive rock formation that pierced the desert with two rock spines that reminded him of monstrous tombstones placed side-by-side touching each other.

"You may know this as Shiprock, but to my people, the Dine', it's known as Tsi' Bit' a' i, the rock with wings. It's sacred to us Navajo people. The old ones tell of how we were brought here from our home in the northlands to this new land."

Tom said, "I can't say I ever saw anything quite like it. We have a place in West Virginia where the rocks shoot straight up out of the mountain, called Seneca Rocks, but nothing quite like this."

"The white man forced us off this land when they thought there was gold here, but there was none."

Tom said, "Seems like wherever there's gold, there's also trouble. The Cherokee were forced off their land in the Appalachian Mountains for the same reason."

Dark Cloud nodded his head. "They offered us land by the river they said was good for growing things, but we chose to come back to this place, Dine'tah, the Land of the People, the Navajo." He paused for a long moment. "Now, sit here and think. It's good for the soul."

Tom sat down and looked out at the stark beauty in front of him. The desert seemed to call out for him to absorb all and become part of it.

They were silent for about five minutes before Dark Cloud spoke. "It was here I came after the war when my head was filled with sights of horrors no man should ever see. It was here the elders of the tribe performed the Enemy Way ceremony to cleanse me from all I'd experienced. And it was here I came to weep when my wife was killed by a drunk driver."

Tom said nothing.

"I belong to this land, Dine'tah, the home of my ancestors."

"This place is incredible," said Tom. "I understand why your people would fight so long and hard for it."

"That's very true, and there's something else I must tell you."

"What?"

"Besides all of this, I must tell you that this rock is hard and cold, and my butt hurts. Come, the night will soon be here, and I have one more thing to show you."

Tom said, "I was getting a little cold, too, but this place certainly can calm the spirit."

Dark Cloud nodded. "We must go," and he was off down the trail.

They made it back to the van much quicker. Tom drove to the gate, Dark Cloud opened it for them, and they were soon on the highway. Tom plowed through the drift, navigated the hairpin turns, and descending the red rock valley to Lukachukai. They passed only one truck going the other way. Dark Cloud spoke, "The road will turn slightly right soon, and I want you to take the trail on the left."

"Okay."

Tom found the trail, which was little more than two parallel ruts. It reminded him of the old road going up Knobley Mountain to the field on top in a cove back home on his father's property. The way soon ended at a cliff. Tom pulled to the edge.

"This is it, my home, Lukachukai. It's not much, but I could live nowhere else. This is where I belong."

Tom looked down on the small town consisting mainly of old trailers and prefab houses. He saw a half-completed building that looked abandoned but said nothing.

"Over there," said Dark Cloud, "is the trading post." He pointed. "And over there is the Chapter House." He paused, "And over there is the biggest eyesore in the whole place, but old man Chees's shack would come in a close second. That unfinished building was to be a fire station complete with an ambulance. The government said if we got it half-built, they'd come up with the money to finish it and then equip it." He stopped. "Seems like the Indian always trust the government. We do our part, and then they forget their promises. I wonder if we'll ever learn. Probably not. And over there," he pointed, "is the grave of my son, Christopher. We'll go there to greet the dawn tomorrow."

After a long minute, Dark Cloud spoke again, "It's getting late, and Sarah will think I've gotten lost. Let's go."

"Whatever you say, Chief."

Dark Cloud looked at Tom and said, "Please don't call me that. A chief is a special person, and I am not he."

"Sorry. I meant no harm. I was only trying to let you know I appreciate what you've done for me today."

"I knew you meant no harm. I've been around some insensitive white people who'd do it to irritate me because I was an Indian. Tom, I felt you meant no harm, but I just wanted to tell you how an Indian feels about it. Let's say no more about this. Let's get down to my house. I think I can smell Sarah's mutton stew from here, and I want you to meet her."

Tom backed up the van and turned it around. The rutted road seemed rougher going down. They made it to the paved road and soon were in front of Dark Cloud's humble home two doors over from the Chapter House. An old GMC truck was parked just outside the rustic wooden fence that had seen better days. They exited the truck and walked to the house. Dark Cloud opened the door, and the smell of stew filled their nostrils.

"Dad, is that you?" called a female voice from the kitchen in the back.

"Yeah, it's me, and I have someone I want you to meet."

A young woman looking to be about 18 years of age walked into the living room. She had dark hair with a hint of auburn and a smile that lit up the room. She stopped when she saw Tom, and the smile got even bigger. "Ya'at'eeh," she said.

Standing in front of Tom was one of the most beautiful women he had ever seen, even wearing faded blue jeans, a flannel shirt, and an apron with flour on it. His heart skipped a beat. "Ya'at'eeh, hello to you, too."

"Tom, this is my daughter, Sarah, and Sarah, this is my guest, Tom. He'll be staying with us for supper and overnight."

Tom wasn't sure what the proper way to greet this young woman was, so he held out his hand. "Very pleased to meet you, Miss Sarah." She stuck out her hand and with a firm grip, shook his. *Was it his imagination, or did he feel a tingle of energy pass between them? Probably just static.*

He looked at her, and her eyes widened slightly. *Yes, she felt it, too.* She let go and turned away. It seemed no one spoke for an eternity, but it was only for a few awkward seconds.

Dark Cloud cleared his throat and broke the silence. "Sarah, I was telling Tom what a great cook you are. Is everything about ready?"

"Yes, it is. The stew's done, and the fry bread just came out of the pan. Dinner's ready now." She went into the kitchen and came out with a large dish containing the stew, and then returned with the fry bread on a large plate with a chip. The food smelled very good to hungry Tom. Dark Cloud filled bowls for all three.

Sarah took off the apron and hung it on a nail in the wall just outside of the kitchen. She sat down, and Dark Cloud took her hand to pray. He held out his hand to Tom. Tom wasn't used to this and hesitated slightly before taking his hand. If Dark Cloud noted Tom's reluctance, he said nothing. Dark Cloud began, "Lord, Creator of all things, we thank you for this food on our table. Bless this house and all in it. And Lord, bless our guest with strength and wisdom. You knew that he'd be here today. Help this young man to choose the right path for his life. Be the light that guides his footsteps through this often dark and stormy world. We ask this in Jesus' name. Amen."

Tom heard his lips say, "Amen," as did Sarah's.

He said, “Thank you for that beautiful prayer. Pardon me for saying so, but I was surprised to hear you pray to the white man’s god. Tell me how you mix your tribe’s beliefs with Christianity.”

“That’s a good question,” said Dark Cloud. You’re not the first to ask it. First off, there’s a hole in every man’s heart, white man, Navajo, or whatever, and can only be filled with Jesus. He came to save the whole world, all of us, be they the white man, the yellow man, the black man, or the red man. I just wish more of the white men who showed us these things would practice what they preach. It would be a far better world.”

Tom nodded his head as he pondered this.

Dark Cloud went on, “While there are differences, there are also many things that are the same. Christians believe in Adam and Eve. Navajo beliefs have a First Man and First Woman. Both believe the world was once destroyed by water covering it. There are other things also, but I’m hungry, so let’s eat before this gets cold.”

Sarah chimed in, “I was about to say the same. You two can discuss religion and any politics later.”

Both men smiled at the mild chastisement and began to eat. Tom found the mutton stew with hominy to be somewhat bland, and he added salt and pepper. The fry bread wasn’t something he’d want seconds of. He ate the piece he’d been given without comment. The coffee was bitter, but he drank it just the same.

After they had finished and cleaned off the table, Tom offered to help Sarah with the dishes. She accepted, and the two made small talk as one washed and the other dried. Tom explained how back home it was only him and his dad, and he was used to doing this task. He noticed how charming and attractive she was, and he also saw how Dark Cloud was watching the two of them from the corner of his eye, though his expression didn't change. When they finished, they took a seat on the sofa across from Dark Cloud.

"So, how did you like your dinner, Tom?" asked Dark Cloud.

"It was a little different from what I'm used to."

"Chris wrote in one of his letters while he was stateside that army food was filling and spicy. I bet you found the mutton stew somewhat bland."

"Well, yes I did, but the salt and pepper helped. Guess fry bread is an acquired taste too."

"It is. For us, it's comfort food." He paused. "I'm glad you came. Sarah, Tom was a soldier in Vietnam, and he and Chris were friends. He was with Chris when he died. I've asked him to come with us at dawn tomorrow to Chris's grave and tell us about his time with him and how he died."

Sarah looked a little surprised and said, "Thank you for coming. We've many questions, and your story will give us answers about our brother and son."

Tom dropped his head. "I'm ashamed to say I almost didn't come. I knew this would be very hard for you and for me, but I'm glad I came, too."

No one spoke for a few moments. Dark Cloud broke the silence. "Tom, you and I talked down at the Charter House about ourselves, but Sarah knows little about you. How about you two get to know each other? I just remembered something I need to do at the Charter House. I'll be back in a little while." With that, he got up, grabbed a coat, and left the house. A cold blast came in as he exited.

The wind slammed the door shut, and the two young people were alone. Sarah said, "This is a little awkward."

Tom shifted in his seat. "Yeah. It is."

"So Tom, tell me about yourself."

"Well, I don't think there's anything special about myself. I grew up in West Virginia, son of a farmer who had to drive a school bus to help make ends meet. I just graduated high school and went into the military where I met your brother."

Sarah said, "A lot of young men here on the Rez do the same. They put in their time and then have GI benefits for life. Chris came from a long line of men who were warriors. When the Navajo Nation made peace with the US government, they pledged never to fight it again. Now they fight with distinction for it."

"I was fortunate to have your brother watching my back."

She said, "This may be hard to understand for you, but Navajo's have an entirely different way of looking at family relationships. They're matriarchal, while white society is patriarchal. Chris was my mother's sister's son." Tom looked somewhat puzzled. She went on. "Let's just say he was my first cousin. My mother was a party girl who drank a lot. About the only thing she did right was when she found out she was pregnant with me; she quit drinking. We have so many kids here born with fetal alcohol syndrome."

"You don't need to be telling me all this."

"No, I do. It's part of who I am. I'm so thankful to be alive and with my uncle, who I call my father. I never knew who my real father was. He may even have been a white man. I don't know." She paused, looked away, smiled, and continued. "When I was a baby, just a month old, one winter night, my mother who was very drunk that night, dropped me off here saying she couldn't care for me. She staggered off in the dark, and they couldn't find her in the driving snow. The next day, they did locate her frozen to death lying out in a cornfield. I guess I could be mad about my beginnings, but I chose to look at what I have, not what I lost. They adopted me before an Arizona state judge, and that's why I call my uncle, father. He's the only father I've ever known."

Tom felt tongue-tied but managed to speak. "That's quite a story. I wish I could be so accepting and confident things will work out. Let me tell you a story. My mother was either a full-blood or half-blood Cherokee from North Carolina. She died when I was young. I still miss those eyes so full of love. She had female cancer and went fast. I only found out about the Cherokee thing a few months ago. You see, back where I come from, there can be a stigma on people with mixed blood."

"Here, too. I know how you feel."

"You know what's funny?"

"No. What? What's funny?"

"I can remember one day when I was shooting the bull with Chris; he said he'd like me to meet his sister. You know how guys are when they're messin' with each other. I never thought it would happen and put it out of my mind till now."

She smiled, "I'm glad we were able to meet. Chris was my protector in school, and for him to say that, I know he thought highly of you." She moved closer to him.

"I, too, am glad we met, but I'm planning on leaving tomorrow. I told my dad I'd be home soon." Tom thought he saw her face drop slightly, though he was sure she tried not to show it. *I wouldn't mind staying here longer, too, and I would if I hadn't told dad when I'd be returning. Don't know how welcome this white boy is on this reservation.* He moved closer.

The front door opened, and again, a gust of cold air poured in as Dark Cloud entered the house. "Sorry I took so long. Several calls came in on the answering machine after I left, and I needed to take care of them. Sarah, Padre over at the church wants to see you at nine. He needs some more information for that daycare job you applied for. Sure is cold. The weatherman on that new Christian radio station, KHAC, says the weather will break about midnight, and then be warmer and calmer for some time." Dark Cloud looked at the two who had moved apart. "What? Did I interrupt something?"

There was silence for a few moments before Sarah spoke, "We were telling each other about our families and growing up."

Dark Cloud looked at them with a degree of suspicion. "That's good," he said hesitantly. "You two seem to have hit it off okay." He smiled a little smirky smile. "We need to get to bed. Getting up to meet the dawn will come very early. We'll get up about five, have some breakfast, and get over to the cemetery about six. Tom, the couch pulls out into a hide-a-bed, so let's all be hitting the sack."

Little more was said that night among them. After all made trips to the bathroom, the lights were turned out, and Tom could hear Dark Cloud snoring. The old sofa bed had seen better days. Tom felt every lump and broken spring, but he was tired. It had been a long and interesting day. Before long, he too was sound asleep.

Chapter 19

3 AM, Next Morning

"***Incoming! Get down!***" screamed Tom as he rolled from the bed and crawled under it. "***Incoming!!***"

Dark Cloud turned on the living room light. He wore only his underwear and looked around, trying to figure what all the commotion was about. Sarah, half asleep and confused, appeared from her room with a robe around her.

"***Incoming! Getdown!***"

Sarah asked her father, "What's wrong with him? Why is he yelling?"

"I've seen this before in soldiers just coming back from war. It's called battle fatigue."

She stepped forward toward him. "We need to help."

Dark Cloud grabbed her by the arm. "No, don't. In his condition, he might think you're the enemy and hurt you. I've heard stories of guys punching their wives when they tried to wake them during their nightmares."

"***Incoming!***"

Dark Cloud and Sarah knelt on the floor. "Tom," he said, but got no response. "Tom," he repeated. "Tom."

Tom groaned but continued to lie under the bed, but Dark Cloud could see that his body was starting to relax. Dark Cloud said, "Tom, wake up. You're having a nightmare."

Tom looked around and saw Dark Cloud and Sarah staring at him. He tried to raise up, but the sofa bed stopped him.

"Tom, you're here with us, Dark Cloud and Sarah," reassured Dark Cloud.

Not again. Tom crawled out from under the bed and sat on it.

"Are you okay?" asked Sarah.

"I think so. What happened?"

Dark Cloud spoke, "You were having a nightmare. I think you were dreaming you were back in Vietnam under attack in the battle."

Tom nodded his head. "Yeah, I think you're right." He said nothing for a few seconds. "Lotta weird stuff been happenin' to me lately."

Dark Cloud asked, "Do you want to tell me about it?"

Tom nodded. "Sometimes, I wonder if I'm going crazy. It started in San Francisco, Chinatown. A bunch of kids threw down some firecrackers, and I hit the ground. They all looked like gooks, and I got up and ran. And then in the desert in Utah, I met and talked to a man who'd been dead for a year. He convinced me to come here when I didn't want to. He said I could give you closure on your son's death." He stopped. "I wish that was all, but I saw some things that were there, and then they weren't near Monument Valley, and now this."

Dark Cloud said nothing as he rubbed his chin thoughtfully. "Sounds like battle fatigue to me. I seen it before. Had a bit of it myself, you know, when I came back from the war in the Pacific."

Tom nodded in agreement. "Yeah, I think so, too."

Sarah said nothing while the two men talked.

Dark Cloud spoke, "I'd have said it could have been a chindi you saw in the desert, but this one was helpful. Chindi are bad medicine, so it must have been some kind of a ministering spirit."

"Ministering spirit?"

"You may have had a visit from one of the Holy People. They're good and created us, or it may have been an angel like the Christians believe in."

"Don't know what it was, but it sure seemed real. It didn't seem like a dream, but I sure can't make sense of it."

Dark Cloud nodded. "Some things are difficult to understand, but I know battle fatigue when I see it."

Tom ran his fingers through his hair and said, "Sorry I scared you guys."

Dark Cloud said, "It's okay. Maybe that spirit angel sent you here so we could help you, too."

"Maybe he did. Looks like I can use all the help I can get."

Sarah finally spoke, "You think you'll be all right now? The morning's coming soon."

"Yeah, I think I'll be okay," said Tom. He looked at Sarah and smiled. She returned his smile.

"Okay," said Dark Cloud. "As Sarah has reminded us, morning's coming, and we still need some more rest." He looked at Tom and asked, "You sure you'll be all right and ready for what we need to do tomorrow?"

Tom nodded his head, "Yeah, I think I'll be all right. Thank you for your understanding. Good night."

In unison, Sarah and Dark Cloud said, "Good night."

Dark Cloud turned off the light switch, and darkness filled the room. Tom lay in bed and tried to sleep. Things weren't making sense, but in his head, he could hear his father's voice: "It'll all work out. Somehow, it will all work out." Those words comforted him. He heard Dark Cloud and Sarah snoring. About ten minutes later, he drifted off to sleep and dreamed dreams of better days when he was a young boy without a care in the world.

Chapter 20

The smell of bacon cooking tickled the nose of sleeping Tom. He opened one eye and checked his watch, 5:00 AM. He rubbed the sleepers from his eyes and looked around the place. Yes, he was still at Dark Cloud's home on the reservation and not in Vietnam. *Thank God.* He'd had another bad dream. He slipped his pants on and noticed light coming from the kitchen. When he opened the door, he startled Sarah, who jumped back.

Tom said, "I'm sorry I frightened you. I saw the light and smelled something cooking, so I came to investigate."

Sarah's face turned from surprise to a little smile. "You did frighten me now, and last night."

Tom grimaced. "Yeah, I've been denying that anything's wrong, but after last night, I believe your dad's right. I've got battle fatigue. I hope I can get over it soon. Enough bad talk, this kitchen sure smells like home. Anything I can do to help?"

She said, "The eggs are done. I hope you like scrambled. Could you make some coffee? The pot is over there."

Tom followed her gaze and saw an old Mr. Coffee. The pot still had about a half-cup left in it. He started to dump this, but Sarah stopped him. "We always save the coffee. Very little gets thrown away here."

Tom looked at her curiously and asked, "Doesn't that make it bitter?"

Sarah nodded her head. “Welcome to the world of Navajo coffee. If you spend much time on the Rez, you’ll get used to it.”

Tom smiled as he looked at her and said, “There’s a number of things I could get used to if I spent more time here.”

Sarah gave him a coy smile as she placed the last of the bacon on a plate and then poured the grease into a jar next to the stove. Several drops splashed on her hand, and she let out a little cry.

“Are you okay?” He put his hand on her arm.

She said, “It will sting a little. I’ll put something on it, and yes, I’m okay.” She smiled as she looked into his eyes. He returned the smile.

The door to the kitchen open with a little screech, and a sleepy-eyed Dark Cloud appeared.

He said, “Hey, I know it’s time to get up, but you two sounded like a cross between magpies and lovebirds.”

They grimaced at this. Tom said, “Sorry to wake you again.”

Dark Cloud said, “No need to apologize. Let’s get this breakfast on the table and eat it. I’ll get the coffee and leftover fry bread. We have important things to do today.”

And so they did. After a quick prayer, the hungry trio wolfed down the morning meal. The dishes went into the sink for cleaning later.

Tom said, “This seemed like a breakfast I get back home, except for the fry bread and coffee.”

Dark Cloud smiled, “You were expecting a slab of buffalo eaten with our fingers?”

"No. It just brought back memories of home. I need to get back to West Virginia soon. My dad's in the early stages of Parkinson's. That's one of the reasons they let me out of the Army. He's gonna need me."

"Just trying to make a joke about the buffalo meat. So many white people still think all Indians still live in teepees and run around saying, Ugh and How. Too many cowboy western movies. Hey, I once met and worked with John Wayne and John Ford on a movie filmed here on the Big Rez."

Sarah interrupted. "Dad, you're not going to tell him **that** story, are you?"

"Why not?" Sarah rolled her eyes as a devilish smile came to her father's face. "Seems in the movie, the Indian's chief, that was me, and cowboys were talking through an interpreter. The interpreter had written lines, but they told me to make up lines in Navajo for my part, so I had a little fun with the cowboys. I said they all wore women's dresses and underwear, were as ugly as buffaloes, and their manhood was so small you needed a magnifying glass to find it. They didn't know the difference, but it about ruined the scene as the other Navajos there in the scene could hardly keep from laughing."

Tom laughed, too, as Sarah rolled her eyes again. Dark Cloud was a character, and Tom liked that.

Dark Cloud continued, "Tom, if you want to call your dad, you can use the phone at the Charter House. There still aren't many on the Rez, so we use smoke signals to communicate. It's rough on a windy day."

Tom laughed again, and Dark Cloud said, "I better shut up. Dawn's coming, and we have to be at the cemetery."

This brought the trio back to earth. They grabbed their coats and hats, left the warm house, and walked the short distance to the cemetery. The weatherman was right. A front had passed overnight, and it was now warmer and calm. A dim light appeared on the eastern horizon. As it brightened, a few scattered clouds became a beautiful orange-red color. They walked through the old gate of the cemetery. There were a few tombstones, but most of the graves had simple wooden crosses. They walked to one that read, Chris Benally, that had some faded plastic flowers attached to it. They stopped at the mounded-up yellowish earth. All three remained quiet for a minute or so. Tom uneasily shifted his weight on his heels.

Dark Cloud looked to the sun about to appear on the horizon, raised his hands, and spoke. “Oh, Great Spirit, Whose voice I hear in the wind, Whose breath gives life to all on this earth. Hear me; I need Your strength and wisdom.”

“Let me walk in beauty. Let it walk before me and behind me. Let it walk above me and beneath me. Beauty is on every side. As I walk, I walk with beauty.

“Make my eyes ever behold the red and purple sunset. Make my hands respect all You have made and my ears sharp to hear Your voice. Give me wisdom to understand the many things as You teach Your people. Keep me strong and calm in the face of all that comes toward me.

“Help me to learn the lessons You hid in every leaf and rock. Let me seek pure thoughts and help others. Help me to find compassion without empathy overwhelming me. Give me strength, not to be greater than another, but to fight my greatest enemy, Me.

“Make me always ready to come to You with my hands clean and my eyes straight.”

Dark Cloud lowered his hands and looked at his son's grave. "And so when life fades as the sunset fades, my spirit may come to You without shame. Amen."

Tom and Sarah said in unison, "Amen."

Dark Cloud looked over to Tom, "Would you now, please tell us about the time you and Chris served together in the Army?"

"Okay." He tried to clear his throat unsuccessfully. He tried again, this time and succeeded. "I met your son and brother on my first day at Fort Benning, Georgia. For reasons only the Army knows, they had all of us digging foxholes in a swamp. I was paired with Chris, and we tried, as did the rest, to make a hole. By noon, everyone including our drill sergeants was covered with this thick, gumbo mud. We got C rations for lunch that must have been left over from World War I. In the afternoon, a monsoon of a thunderstorm came up. It made the swamp muddier if that was possible, but it did rinse most of the mud off us, at least to our knees. Finally, someone with a lick of sense realized that all the lightning could kill us off before we ever got to face the enemy, and we were ordered onto an old Bluebird bus. It was pretty trashed out. It was obvious this wasn't the first time this bus had a bunch of soaked and muddy soldiers in it. The rain poured for over an hour, and I had a lot of time to talk with Chris. He took up most of the seat, by the way. Don't know if this exercise was to bond us or not, but it sure did. We all, including the drill sergeants, hated whoever was behind this crazy exercise.

"I met another fellow, a black man from a neighboring town back home, named Bill Hairston, and he rounded out our usual group. We hung around together and watched each other's back when we went to town. The town near the base in Vietnam wasn't much, smelly and dirty, a good place a GI could get a knife in his back for his paycheck. We hit the bars to try to drown our sorrows of being in this hellhole. There was every kind of deviant entertainment in that stinking village, but we only hit the bars, and then the Three Amigos staggered home together." Tom could see Dark Cloud knew precisely what he was hinting at and, he also noticed a sigh of relief when he said they did not partake of the available entertainment.

"We weren't there long when word circulated through the men that a bigwig general wanted to find the enemy and engage them, so we were sent into western Vietnam to the Ia Drang valley. They thought the enemy was there and boy, oh boy, were they right. I think we found the whole regular North Vietnamese Army. Horribly outnumbered, we fought for our lives. Death and destruction were all around us as bullets flew, mortars howled, and jets dropped bombs and napalm." Tom paused for a moment. "Our friend, Bill, died the first day in the afternoon. I was there with him too, when he died. I've often wondered if I should tell his family what happened like I'm telling you now." Tom looked at Dark Cloud, who nodded a yes. Sarah stood stoically nearby, but Tom could also see she nodded slightly also.

"The next day was hell-on-earth. It was more like the first day, only worse because we were so tired. I don't think anyone slept. It was a full moon, a Hunter's Moon. Going into this, we thought we were the hunters, but now we were the hunted. We were just trying to stay alive. The helicopters, Hueys, came in with much-needed supplies, mainly ammo, and carried the dead and wounded out. Without the Hueys' support, we'd been overrun several times. Somehow, we two got through day two of the battle with only ant bites and a few minor cuts from a grass with razor-like leaves.

"We got no sleep that night either as the enemy tried to sneak up on us under cover of darkness. The full moon gave them away, and we fired off illumination flares that lit up the area. They were right upon us, and we mowed them down with 50 calibers and our M16s. They attacked at dawn again. We were so hungry and thirsty and worn out, but to quit was to die. Everyone, no matter how tired, had to keep going, and we did somehow.

"Around two in the afternoon under heavy fire, the Hueys returned with more ammo and removed the dead and wounded. Our sergeant yelled for Chris and me to help with the tasks which we did. The cargo area floor was covered with blood from the bleeding men." Tom stopped for a moment. *What was that? It sounds like, it can't be, but it was.* Tom heard the distinct thud-thud-thud sound the rotors of a Huey makes. The noise got closer and louder. Thud-thud-thud it went, and as he turned his head, he saw the Hueys coming from the north right at them. *Was he hallucinating? Were they really there?*

He turned to face them, nearly stumbled and fell, but Dark Cloud grabbed his arm and held him up. He knew what Tom was thinking. "They're real, Tom. They're real. I can see them, too." Sarah went to Tom and thrust her arm under his arm to help hold him up. He looked at her, and a little smile came to his face that Dark Cloud noticed. The thud-thud-thud got louder as the choppers approached and went directly overhead. They became smaller as they continued south, becoming a dots that disappeared, though the thud-thud-thud of the rotors could still be heard faintly. This, too, soon went away.

They looked to the south for a few more moments. Tom regained his composure and began to feel awkward. The other two picked up on this and gently let go of his arms. Relieved, he continued. "As we were loading the dead and wounded into the chopper, I got hit. There was blood everywhere and pain like I'd never felt. The chopper was almost full when Chris threw me into the space left. As he did this, he took several rounds in his torso. With what strength I had left, I pulled him into the chopper, and he fell on top of me. We were nose to nose, and I could feel his warm blood pouring onto me. He looked me eye-to-eye and said, 'Tom,

I'm dying.' I lied to him and said he wasn't, but we knew he was. He said again, 'I'm dying.' His face twisted with pain, and he said, 'Promise me this, Tom, promise me this. You'll tell my father that I died in battle.' I said I would, and then his face dropped, and his empty eyes just stared into mine. I closed my eyes and began to cry. That's the last I remember till I woke up in a hospital. I asked about Chris, but no one seemed to know anything about him. They did a little checking for me and found out he hadn't made it. I didn't want to come here with this news, and you knew I almost didn't."

Dark Cloud said, "I'm glad you did. It gives me closure, and now I know my son died the good death of a warrior." A small smile came to his face.

Sarah added, "Tom, I'm glad you came and shared this with us. No one should die alone without a friend. I'm glad you were there." She went over to Tom and slipped her arm around his.

Tom nodded but could say nothing. No one spoke for what seemed an eternity but was just a few moments. Finally, Dark Cloud raised his hands to the sky and began to pray. "Live your life, so the fear of death can never enter your heart. Love your life, perfect your life, and beautify all things in your life. Seek to make your life long and be a service to your people. Prepare a noble death song for the day you go over the great divide. When you arise in the morning, give thanks for the light, for your life and strength. Give thanks for your food and the joy of living. If you see no reason for giving thanks, the fault is yours.

"When your time comes to die, be not like those whose hearts are filled with the fear of death, so that when their time comes, they weep and pray for more time to live their lives over again in a different way. Sing your death song, and die like a hero coming home." He lowered his hands and said, "Amen."

In unison, Tom and Sarah said, "Amen."

No one said anything. The sound of the wind blowing through the sagebrush was the only thing that broke the silence. A full minute passed before Dark Cloud said to Tom, "Again, thank you for coming. I now know my son died well. That means a lot to me. The People, the Dine', value strength and bravery in our people."

Tom nodded, "He was a good man. I wouldn't be here today if not for him. I want to stay here and talk to him alone. I still have a few things I need to say."

"Okay," said Dark Cloud. He turned to Sarah, "Oh, don't forget, the padre over at the church needed to talk with you about that job at the daycare. His call came in last night while I was at the Charter House. Remember? I told you last night."

"Let's go and leave Tom to say what he needs to, and we'll meet him back at our house. That good with you, Tom?"

"Yes, it is. I'll be there shortly."

Dark Cloud and Sarah turned toward their home and were soon gone. Tom sat on the cold, red earth next to the new grave. "Well, old buddy, if anyone had told me a year ago I'd be sitting next to a grave of my best friend in the cold desert of Arizona, I'd have told them they were crazy, but here I am. It's hard to believe you can become so close to another person in such a short time, but it happens." A tear ran from his eye down his cheek. "Why I'm not six feet under, and you are, I'll never know. It seems like if anyone should have died, it should have been me." Tom was still for a moment. "Thank you for being my friend and showing me sacrificial love. I hope I can be half the man you were."

The words barely left his mouth when Tom's eyes filled with tears. He began to cry so hard his body shook. When he could weep no more, Tom wiped the wetness from his eyes and face and stood up. He reached in his pocket, pulled out some change, and laid a quarter on the small grave marker. "Chris, this is to say I was with you when you died. I was proud to serve with you. May you be at peace with your ancestors." He slowly turned and began to walk away but turned back to the new grave. "Goodbye, my friend. Till we meet again."

He headed toward Dark Cloud's humble home. The cold and wind bit at his exposed skin. *So much for the day feeling warmer. Maybe it was just him.* He pulled the collar up around his neck and wished he had gloves to warm his icy fingers. The frozen ground crunched. Soon, he arrived in town, went down a short unpaved street, and found Dark Cloud's home. Tom knocked on the door. No one answered. He tried the cold doorknob, which turned in his even colder hand. Tom walked into the warm house and sat down. He was tempted to leave, but couldn't bring himself to do this without at least saying goodbye.

Ten minutes passed before Dark Cloud, and Sarah entered the house. "Man, oh man. It sure is cold out there," said Dark Cloud. "Glad the weatherman says it's going to warm up. I think they call it 'Indian summer' where you come from. Whatever it's called, I'll take it."

"Me, too," said Tom. "I want to thank you for all the kind hospitality you've shown me. Sorry, I scared you so last night."

Dark Cloud said, "I've meant to talk with you about that. I've seen it in lots of soldiers just home from war. We called it battle fatigue, but I think they're going to change the name of this condition to Post Traumatic Stress Disorder or PTSD. Either way, I'd like to help. I had it after the Big War. What helped me was time up on the mountain where I took you, and the singers who did the 'Enemy Way' ceremony for me. I'd like you to stay. Go up on the mountain where I found needed rest from the war. You'll find some peace there like I did."

Sarah said, "I would like you to stay, too."

A look of surprise came to Tom's eyes. He did like it here. The desert had a beauty, unlike the hills of home, and Dark Cloud and Sarah had been so caring. "I don't know what to say. It's so tempting. I don't have any set time to be home, but I'm concerned about my dad. As I told you at breakfast, one of the reasons the Army let me out was his health since he's been diagnosed with Parkinson's disease."

Dark Cloud shook his head. "Again, I'm sorry to hear that. But I'd like you to stay. Tell you what, why don't you give him a phone call and see how he's doing. You can check on things back home. We have a phone at the Chapter House you can use."

Tom thought for a moment. He liked the idea, but he needed to know about his dad. "Okay. If all's well on the home front, I'll stay." A smile came to Sarah's face.

"Good," said Dark Cloud. "Let's go make that call."

All three left the warm home and walked the short distance to the Chapter House. Dark Cloud let them in and directed Tom to the phone in his office. He showed Tom how to get a long-distance line. Tom had his dad in West Virginia on the line in no time, and Dark Cloud left the room to give them some privacy. As Tom talked with his father, he heard Dark Cloud and Sarah talking, but he couldn't make out what they said even if it was in English.

His father was happy to hear from him and glad he was well and with friends. Take your time he said, and enjoy the trip home. There was no need to hurry. He was well and doing fine. The Parkinson's was in the early stage, and it was hardly noticeable. He said the Army had blown it all out of proportion, but just the same, he was glad Tom was back in the USA. They made some small talk about the farm, before saying their goodbyes.

Tom got up from the table and left the room. Dark Cloud and Sarah were waiting for him. "Well?" asked Dark Cloud. "What did he say?"

"He said to take my time, and he was okay."

"Good," said Dark Cloud. "I've good some warm clothes and an arctic sleeping bag I can loan you. Go over to the Trading Post. Get what food you need and fill the bus up with gas. You'll need it. And one more thing. Sarah says she's going with you up on the mountain."

Tom's mouth dropped open, and he weakly said, "Okay."

He looked at Dark Cloud and asked, "Aren't you concerned about the two of us being together alone up there?"

Dark Cloud looked a little surprised. "She is of age and a full-grown woman. Nothing will happen to her that she doesn't want to happen."

Again, Tom was surprised, and another weak okay stumbled from his lips.

They left the Chapter House and headed to Dark Cloud's home. Tom fired up the VW bus and went to the Trading Post and purchased supplies for two, gasoline for the van, and a pair of fur-lined gloves. Back to his host's home, Dark Cloud piled two sleeping bags into the vehicle, and Sarah added two backpacks, one large, one small. The young people got into the van.

Dark Cloud said, "If anyone gives you trouble up on the mountain, which is unlikely this time of year, tell them you're an

Indian too, and if that isn't enough, tell them you've got permission from Hosteen Benally. Everyone knows me."

Tom looked at Sarah, who grimaced. She'd told her dad about his ancestry. "Thanks. Will do," and a few minutes later, he drove up the twisting road to Buffalo Pass. The heater on the van slowly warmed the vehicle. Tom looked over at Sarah, who smiled.

I must be dreaming. Am I really in the middle of nowhere Arizona going camping with a beautiful girl I barely know? Yeah, I must be dreaming, but he secretly hoped he wasn't. He'd enjoy it as long as it lasted.

Chapter 21

Tom awoke from restful sleep. Light from the moon shone through the windows of the VW bus. The air inside was crisp and cold, and he saw his breath. *Where am I? Vietnam? Home in West Virginia*? He heard a soft sigh from the person lying next to him. Her warm body touched his, and he remembered. He'd been on this majestic mountain with a beautiful young woman for the last week. It seemed like an unbelievable, beautiful dream. He looked at his watch, 5:00 AM. He turned his head to the east and saw a trace of light on the horizon.

The young, half-asleep woman spoke, "You have a bad dream, or are you getting up?"

"No bad dreams. Think I'll get up and greet the dawn. How about you, Sarah?"

In the moonlight, he saw her stretch and yawn. She smiled and said, "Think I want to sleep a little longer. Why don't you go to the point, and I'll meet you there in a while? Got my watch set for 5:45, so I don't miss the dawn." She raised herself on one elbow and leaned forward for a kiss. Tom happily met her lips. "Go ahead. I'll be there shortly."

"Okay. I'll do that. It'll give me some time to think."

She smiled, pulled the sleeping bag up to her neck. "Okay. See you at the crack of dawn." She covered her head up with the cloth, wiggled a little to get comfortable, and her breathing became slow and rhythmic.

Tom looked at the sleeping woman next to him. *How easy it was for her to go to sleep and how easy it had been for him this week to get to sleep and stay asleep lying next to her.* Many nights since leaving Vietnam hadn't been like that. Carefully, he put his pants and flannel shirt on. He had his socks on already. Cold feet at night were no fun. He pulled the laces on the heavy work shoes uptight and tied them in a bow as he tried not to disturb the sleeping woman next to him. Tom grabbed his heavy coat from the back of the passenger's seat and put it on. It was as cold as the air in the van, and it made him shiver. The van auxiliary heater quit working on the second night, and they were thankful for the heavy sleeping bags. Tom smiled to himself. It was another reason to get close to her. The shared body heat in the sleeping bags kept them from freezing in the cold VW van, and she seemed to enjoy the snuggle time. He knew he did.

The coat now felt warm. Tom unlocked the side door and gently slid it open. The ground crunched as he stepped out. He exited swiftly, depressed the door lock, and gently closed the door. Sarah didn't stir in her cocoon. The last thing he wanted was to have her awaken. *Mission accomplished.* He turned to the east and saw his warm breath in the pale morning light. The sky was showed a growing pale yellow on the far horizon. A short jaunt took him to the rocky point jutting out from the mountain.

Each morning for the last six days, they'd met the dawning here. Part of him wanted her with him now, but more of him was glad she hadn't come yet. He'd have alone time to think about Sarah and the last week. Never had he met a girl like her, so full of life and so sweet, but wise beyond her years. She seemed a little naïve about some things outside of the reservation, but he noted how well she read him, and that quality would be very useful for her and whatever husband she would choose. *Husband! What was he thinking?* He mulled this idea around in his head. *Could she possibly be the one for him?* They came from such different backgrounds. Her world was the Big Reservation. His was the old farmhouse at the base of Knobley Mountain and 100 miles in all directions with Cumberland, Maryland, at the center, but it was now bigger. He'd seen more of the big world, and he liked it. *Could she adjust to his world?* There was no way he would feel at home in this high and dry desert. He'd miss the green hills; he was sure of that. *Could she live in his world? Did she even want him with such a commitment?* Still, the way she looked at him spoke volumes.

She was so beautiful, so pleasant to be around. He didn't see Sarah as a girl who'd throw herself at a man. They had kissed passionately, and her body felt so good touching his. He wanted her in more ways than one. He'd seen no desire to stop in her eyes or actions, but he stopped when he thought of his war injury. *Could she accept him maimed as he was in body and mind?* Tom pondered this. He was far from perfection in many ways.

Some people thought gold was the perfect thing to have, but all that glittered wasn't gold. People bleed and died to have it. It seemed to cause trouble wherever it was or even was thought to be. The Navajos weren't the only ones it had brought problems to. They'd been forced from their homes because of its empty promises. Perhaps people were better off without it. *How many had been destroyed by it*? For some, it seemed an addiction no more fulfilling than chasing the wind.

Maybe perfection on earth wasn't a good thing on this imperfect earth. These thoughts troubled his sleep-fogged mind. The sunrise should bring some clarity to the new day, a gift from the Creator, Dark Cloud had called it.

Tom looked to the eastern sky and saw a cloud blocking the sun's light. He glanced at his watch, 7:00 AM. *Had he been here that long lost in thought, and where was Sarah? She should have been here some time ago.*

The distant noise caught his attention. *Was it Sarah?* If it was an Indian, he or she wasn't trying to sneak up on him. It was hard to see for the small ponderosa and pinyon pines blocking his view. The person came closer, and Tom was pleased to see it was Sarah. "I'm over here," he yelled.

"Be right there. Give me a minute," she hollered back.

She made her way to the rocky outcropping where Tom sat. "Hello, handsome. Mind if I pull up a rock next to you?"

"You can pull up any rock in the house you wish, but I just have one question."

"And what's that?"

Tom did his best Humphrey Bogart imitation. "Here's lookin' at you, kid. Kiss me as if it were the last time."

She smiled, closed her eyes, and puckered her lips for a kiss. Their lips locked passionately for a long time. When it was over, Sarah smiled and asked, "Do you want me to round up the usual suspects?"

"Ah, Casablanca. I see you're an old movie fan."

"Old movies are all we ever see out here on the reservation."

Tom smiled at her little joke, and she returned it. The rising sun touched Shiprock brightly illuminated it, And the immense rock casts a long, dark shadow toward Tom and Sarah. She wrapped her arm around Tom's back. They sat this way just enjoying the sunrise and each other's company. "Beautiful, isn't it?" she said.

"Yes. I can see why Dark Cloud showed me this location he loved. If this doesn't bring peace to your soul, I don't know what will."

"And beauty," said Sarah.

Tom nodded his head, "And beauty."

A cold wind picked up and whipped at the old, woolen army blanket the two had wrapped around them. Neither said much as they watched the day awaken. They huddled together, simply enjoying their time together and the shared body heat. Tom wanted to pinch himself to see if his good fortune was real or a dream. Sarah caught his eye and smiled as she had many times this week. Tom coyly smiled back, and Sarah glanced away toward Shiprock. She said, "My people, the Dine', say the peak we call Tse'Bit'a'i' was once a great bird that brought the Navajo from the north to their new home here. We consider it sacred. There are many other legends concerning Tse'Bit'a'i'."

"It's very beautiful and tranquil on this mountain." He paused. "Back home in West Virginia, I have a mountain like this. Whenever I need to be alone and think, I'd climb to the top of Knobley Mountain behind my home. It seemed like the air was always fresher up there. When I came down, I always felt refreshed."

She looked in his eyes and nodded. "After the only mother I knew, Whistling Woman, Dark Cloud's wife, was killed by a drunk driver, he'd bring Chris and me up here when the horrors of the world would close in around us. I think that's how he kept his sanity, that and the fact Chris and me needed him. Somehow, he survived, but it was hard on everyone."

"My mom died from cancer when I was young. Sometimes, I'd climb to the top of that mountain and cry. Other times, I'd scream at God for taking my mom and then cry. Somehow after that, a sense of peace would come to me, and I'd be okay till the next time I got mad at the unfairness of the world."

"Yes," said Sarah. "I've been there too many times. Don't seem like neither one of us was born with a silver spoon in our mouths."

"My dad says struggles make us strong," added Tom. "He also says he wished there was another way to achieve this. It seems there's so much pain involved till we have victory. Why were you late? I was expecting you sooner."

"I'm on Indian time." Tom looked at her suspiciously. "It's a common excuse you hear on the Rez for lateness." His look turned to questioning. "Okay, okay, you caught me. I turned off the alarm and fell back asleep."

Tom smiled, "You were missing another incredible sunrise."

"And you didn't."

Tom smiled again. He must be dreaming, and he didn't want to wake up. The couple sat side-by-side touching and not talking for another five minutes until Tom's stomach began to growl. She looked at Tom as it growled again and said, "Tom, I think we better feed that bear before it eats us up."

"You can say that again. Ever since I was little, my stomach's growled that way. I'm getting hungry. Had your fill of beauty from this sunrise?"

"Yes, and now I'd like my fill of breakfast."

"Well, what are we waiting for?" He swung his head in a "let's go" motion, and off they went down to where the VW microbus among the trees. It didn't take long for them to reach their destination. Tom nearly fell on the way but recovered with only his pride hurt.

At the vehicle, they took a two-burner camper stove out and set it up on a rock shaped like a short pillar. Soon, a pot of water boiled, and eggs and bacon cooked. Tom threw some coffee grounds in their cups for "cowboy coffee" and poured in water. Sarah placed the eggs done over easy on the plates with the bacon and put store-bought white bread and jam next to the eggs. The hungry couple chowed down on their breakfast. Tom stirred the coffee and gave a cup to Sarah. She sipped carefully on the hot liquid, and they made small talk.

A sour look came to Tom's face after a sip. "Let me tell you, the grounds on the bottom are bitter. Yuck."

"Taste like Navajo coffee?"

"Yeah, it does."

"Navajos are notorious for bitter coffee. You should know that by now."

Tom said, "So I'm finding out again. Don't think I could get used to it."

"Me neither. It's too bitter that way, and I'd just rather do without sometimes, but Dark Cloud would fuss at me when he caught me pouring old coffee down the drain."

Tom smiled, and a sound on the mountain caught his ear. Far down the road, an old WWII vintage Jeep was approaching. "You expecting someone?"

"No," she replied as the Jeep steadily came closer. When it was about 100 feet away, she said, "I know him. That's Jim Begay. I went to Navajo Nations High School with him. He was on the Redskins, our basketball team. Wonder what he wants?"

"The Redskins?"

"If we can't use the name, who can?"

"Good point," said Tom.

The Jeep rolled to a stop, and a tall, young man with long, black hair tied in a ponytail got out. "Sarah," he said. "Your father asked me to come up here and find you two. I'd have used smoke signals, but you were on the other side of the mountain. He needs to see you. It's important."

Tom looked at Sarah and said, "Smoke signals again?"

Sarah's face had an unpleasant look, "Common old Indian joke, and a poor one at that. Jim, thank you for delivering the message on this cold day. Did he say what it was about?"

"No. He had a somber look on his face when he asked for my help. I wish I could tell you more, but it seemed personal, so I didn't press for details. I hope everything is okay with him."

She said, "Thanks Jim. Tell father we'll be there soon."

"I'll do that. See you in town." He got back into the Jeep, turned it around, and took off down the old road through the forest.

"Tom, I'll clean up breakfast, and you get the van ready for travel."

"Sounds like a plan." Before long, the two were bouncing down the rutted trail toward the main road and wondering what was so critical for Dark Cloud to send a messenger to retrieve them. They'd soon find out.

Chapter 22

The two in the VW microbus spoke little as they rode down the curvy road toward Lukachukai. Each seemed lost in their thoughts. *What could it be? What had happened?*

After maneuvering around a hairpin turn, Tom spoke to Sarah. “Any idea what he has to tell us?”

“No, I don’t. This came like a shot out of the blue. My best and only guess is it has something to do with Dark Cloud, and I fear the worst.”

“I don’t know. Something doesn’t feel right.”

They drove the next few miles down the twisting road in the red rock canyon to the small Indian town and pulled up beside Dark Cloud’s house. They got out and entered the warm abode. After hellos and greeting, Dark Cloud said, “Sit down. I need to talk to both of you.”

Tom’s heart fell inside of him. Dark Cloud said, “Sarah, the padre called and asked if you could start today. Someone up and quit, and he’s short-handed. He said you could start right now, as soon as you got back to town.”

“That’s a surprise, Dad. I thought I’d have some more time.”

Dark Cloud turned and focused his gaze on Tom. “And Tom, this isn’t going to be easy. “I had to make some decisions concerning you. I don’t know if you are going to like them or not, but I tried to do what I thought was best.” He paused, “Tom, yesterday I got a phone call from your father, and we had a long talk." He stopped again. "This really isn't a good way to tell you this. Your father told me that the day before yesterday, after finishing off his bus run taking the school kids home, he tripped and fell on the steps while getting out of the bus. He knew he hurt his leg and ankle, so he called your Uncle Bill, who took him to Memorial Hospital in Cumberland. The x-rays showed he had a badly broken ankle. They set the leg and told him to stay off of it and not drive for six weeks while it heals. Your Uncle Bill took over his bus route the next day, but can't for the remainder of the six weeks. Your dad needs to finish out this year to qualify for his pension. The principal says he'd keep him in the spot if your dad could find a substitute, and he said you could do it until he was well enough to go back to work. Your dad said if he lost this job now to someone else, he'd never get it back and never get that pension he desperately needs."

Tom nodded. Yes, he understood. Jobs were hard to find, and his dad badly needed that small pension. "I'll do it. My dad's always been there for me through thick and thin, and he needs me now." He looked at Dark Cloud. "Any ideas about how I can get from here to West Virginia quickly?"

Dark Cloud gave a little sheepish smile. "I hope I did the right thing. I booked an airline ticket, a red-eye, for you tonight out of Albuquerque to Baltimore. We have to leave within the hour for you to make it."

Sarah sighed. "I wish you didn't have to go, but I know what it's like when the family needs you. You do what you must."

He opened his mouth to speak, but nothing came out. He dropped his eyes, looked at Dark Cloud, and asked, "What about my microbus?"

"I knew you'd get around to that. I'll go with you to the airport and bring it back to the Big Rez. When you have this situation at home under control, come back and get it. I'll keep it safe and sound. I hope by now, you've learned to trust me."

Tom said, "Trusting you is not the problem. I knew real quick like you were an honorable man true to your word. Having this dumped on me all at once is, well, overwhelming. I'd hoped for more time before I had to get off my joy ride and face reality, but duty calls. I'll do what needs to be done."

Dark Cloud cleared his throat and said, "I need to run over to the Chapter House for about a half-hour. Tom, can you have the van like you want to leave it and your things packed for the flight in that time and say your goodbyes?"

"Yes, I can be ready in a half-hour. I sure hate to leave so soon." Tom glanced at Sarah, who returned his gaze.

"Okay," said Dark Cloud. "I'll be gone a half hour and not a minute more. There'll be no Indian time wiggle room. I'll be back shortly," and he left the house.

"You know, Tom, I don't want you to go. I was enjoying having you here so much, but I know I'd do the same if I were in your shoes."

"I don't want to go either, but I must. Dad needs me. He's always been there when I needed him."

"Tom, I want you to know I've never done this with another man before. I so enjoyed being with you these days. At times in the dark, when we hugged and kissed, I wanted you so bad, but you were the perfect gentleman. I've had a few dates where I had to fight my way away from those pawing hands, but not you. I've never met a fellow like you. Wish this dream didn't have to end so soon."

Tom winced when she had said, a perfect gentleman. He so enjoyed his time with her and didn't want it to end. "I'll," he stammered, "I'll be back." He put his arms around her, and she did the same. Lips met, and they kissed like they may never get the chance again, long and hard.

Their lips parted, and Tom said, "I hate to break the spell, but I need to have the van packed up when your father returns."

"I don't want it to end, either. I'd like this not to be the last chapter in our book. I think I want to write more with you in it."

"I'd like that very much, also." They released their loving embrace, and Tom asked, "Do you have an old suitcase I could borrow and some cardboard boxes for the things in the VW?"

"Wait right here." Sarah went into her room and quickly returned with a suitcase with a Beatles picture on the side and several medium size boxes. "This is mine. I used it when the basketball team went to the state championship in Phoenix. It's not so manly, but it's the best I can do."

"Any port in a storm," said Tom. She looked a little puzzled. He explained, "It's something my father always says. It means you take any harbor or shelter in a time of need, even ones you wouldn't normally use."

"Looks like we have much to learn about each other."

"Sounds very interesting," he said, "but if we keep up this yammering, I'll never be ready when Dark Cloud returns."

"Okay, where do we begin?"

"Everything I have is in the van, so let's make like two frogs and hop to it."

She rolled her eyes. "Are you always so corny?"

"Only with girls I'm trying to impress."

Packing didn't take long, and Dark Cloud was back on the dot. "You two ready?"

"As ready as I'm going to be," said Tom.

Sarah sighed, "Me, too. Guess we both have to go."

Dark Cloud said, "Tom, it's a long way, and we can make better time if I drive. I know the road, and there's something a few miles down the road I want to show you. Would you mind if I drove first?"

"No." He handed the keys of the vehicle to Dark Cloud. "Let's go."

The trio piled in the microbus, and Dark Cloud drove to the old church mission where Sarah's new job waited for her. Dark Cloud spoke, "You two can say your goodbyes, but remember, we need to get this young man all the way to Albuquerque today. His flight won't wait."

Tom and Sarah looked at Dark Cloud and smiled. "Okay, we'll try not to take too long."

"Good," said Dark Cloud. "I don't want to have to throw a bucket of water on you to separate you."

Sarah smiled coyly. They exited the van and went in the front door of the mission. A short six feet away was another set of solid double doors. She stopped and turned to Tom. "I guess this is goodbye."

Tom replied, "I guess it is goodbye, for now, anyway. I don't want to leave, but my father needs me."

Dark Cloud pulled the microbus back onto the main road and continued east for about five miles. He took a left on a dirt road and stopped at a rutted, dirt parking area. "What I want to show you is a short distance ahead. We walk from here. Be careful. There's a cliff ahead."

They got out and walked about 1/5 of a mile to a 1,000-foot drop-off. The sun shone down into the deep valley below. "This is Canyon de Chelley. Down in the valley, my people grow corn using water from the small stream."

"You wanted to show me a cornfield?"

"No. Look under the cliffs along the valley for some ruins."

"I see 'em. Stone dwellings similar to the Pueblo structures."

Dark Cloud said, "Those are the dwelling places of the Anasazi, the Ancient Ones. They were here when the Navajos came to this land long ago. They are the places of chinde, spirits, and we leave them alone." He stopped and took a breath. "I told you this before, but it's worth repeating. The whites forced us from this land when they thought there was gold here. Fortunately, there was none, and they lost interest, and we returned to our homeland.

"Two things I want you to remember. Number one, gold and greed can make men behave foolishly, worse than animals." Tom listened intently. "And number two, the Old Ones are gone. Little remains of them. One day, you and I will also be gone. Find beauty wherever you walk and be at peace with God, whatever name you may know Him by. Remember these two things, and you will be ahead of most people."

"I do appreciate that, and I'll remember it, but why did you feel you needed to tell me this?"

Chapter 23

Dark Cloud said, "Why? I felt it in my heart. I believe the Creator of all put it there, and He wanted me to tell you this. You will need to remember and use this message at some time in your life." Dark Cloud looked to the east toward the sun and the valley, raising his hands he intoned. "Oh, Ancient Ones, we didn't come to disturb you, but remember you. Tell the Creator that we're well and soon will be coming." He looked at Tom. "Now, we must go. You have a plane to catch."

As they walked back up to the van, Tom asked, "What did you mean by 'we'll soon be coming'?"

Dark Cloud stopped and faced Tom. "The Ancient Ones walked this land like we do today. They must have thought they'd be here forever. We think life will go on day after day after day, but it won't. All will die. The Ancient Ones are gone. My wife has gone, and my son has gone. We will be gone too soon. Don't get too attached to what does not last. Only the Creator will last. Be at peace with Him and find beauty."

"I'll remember your words."

"Remember and implement them daily in your life, and you'll find peace in a world upside down." Dark Cloud said no more, and the two men walked the remaining distance over the rocky ground to the van.

They got in and said nothing. Each seemed deep in thought. The construction site of the school soon passed, and neither spoke for forty long miles. They drove into the largest town Tom had seen on the reservation. "This is Window Rock. You'll see why shortly. The Navajo Nation council meets and does its work of governing here. There're plans to build a museum to tell the story of the Dine' and Dine'tah." He cleared his throat, "And just across the state line in New Mexico, we'll stop for a bathroom break and some lunch. If I don't find a bathroom soon, I'll need to make like a cow out in the field."

Tom said, "Me, too. My eyes are floating, and my stomach's growling. A stop sounds like a great idea."

Dark Cloud took a right off Route 66 into the Blake's Lotaburger parking lot. Once inside the restaurant, they headed for the bathroom and took care of business. The relieved men left the bathroom after washing their hands. Dark Cloud said, "Tom, find us a table. I can't believe how busy this place is. I'll order."

Tom found an open table near the window and sat down. Dark Cloud came over to the table and sat down. "Where's the food?" Tom asked.

"It'll be here in a few minutes. They cook everything to order. Trust me; the wait will be worth it. I ordered burgers with green chiles, big fries, and Cokes. I hope that's okay with you?"

"Right now, I'm so hungry I could eat my shoe, so anything should taste good. Can't say I ever ate a burger with chiles on it before," Tom said.

"Fellow started this chain in Albuquerque shortly after WWII. People asked for chiles on their burgers, and they'd even bring the chiles in the store and put them on. He tried it, liked it, and added it to the menu. Now when you think of Blake's, people think of that signature chile burger. If you're ever in business, remember that. If people ask for it, and you don't have it, you'd better get it, or someone else will meet the need."

“Sounds like good advice. I’ll remember it.” Tom took a bit of the chile burger. “Say, this is good, but a little hot for my tastes.”

Dark Cloud smiled. “You’ve got gringo taste buds, not used to the burn. I got you the mild. Ever heard of the Scoville Scale?” Tom took another bite and shook his head. “These chiles rate low on it. The little Mexican kids around here eat the ones at the top of the scale like they’re candy. I tried one, and it liked to burned my mouth up.”

Tom wiped some ketchup from his mouth. “I like it. All the same, I think I’ll stick to the low enders.”

“No argument there, Tom.”

The two men finished their meals and got up to leave. The table immediately was taken by four men wearing hard hats. Tom and Dark Cloud worked their way through the packed restaurant to the exit, walked to the van, and were back on Route 66 heading east. Near Gallup, they passed the largest flea market Tom had ever seen. There were on and off-ramps for a new four-lane highway. “This new interstate road will do away with lots of old Route 66,” said Dark Cloud. “A lot of people are sad to see this old road disappear.”

They rode on for a few more minutes. Dark Cloud looked over at Tom and smiled. “You and my daughter sure seemed to hit it off. I’ve never seen her interested in a guy like this before.”

“Yeah, we hit it off real well. I’ve never met a girl like her. She’s something all right.” Tom took a sip of water from the cup he got at Blake’s.

“Dark Cloud asked, “Did you two have sex the week you were together?”

When Tom heard the question, he began to choke on the drink and then cough it up. He drew in some deep breaths and looked at Dark Cloud with a mixture of surprise and concern.

Dark Cloud continued, "The Navajo are a matriarchal tribe as are most in America. Our women have much freedom. Some use it wisely; some don't." He stopped and fixed his gaze on Tom. "I'm sure Sarah has never been with a man before."

Tom stared at the older man. No anger showed in Dark Cloud's eyes, only concern. "Sir, I never had sex with her."

"Why not? I know the look of love when I see it."

Tom cringed. It was time to come clean with Sarah's father. "Dark Cloud, your daughter's an incredible woman, unlike any I've ever met, and we kissed and hugged and all that, and yes, I wanted her and she me, but you see…," he swallowed hard, "I have a problem."

Dark Cloud looked at Tom with suspicion. "What kind of a problem?"

Tom dropped his eyes. "I was wounded in the war." He stopped for a moment and then continued. "In the big battle where your son died, I got shot. I lost one of my testicles." He studied Dark Cloud's stony face. "The docs said I was lucky. Many men lost far more. They said it would have little if any effect on my love life or my ability to become a daddy, and I should consider myself fortunate." He stopped, then started again, "I know all that's true, but I feel disfigured, and I don't know if a woman could accept me as I am."

The two men drove on in silence for a while before Dark Cloud let out a deep breath. "You had me wondering. For a moment, I thought you're going to tell me you liked guys. Look Tom, I understand your reluctance to talk about this matter, but you are lucky. Many men who were in Vietnam would gladly trade places with you. There's a lot more to being a man than whether you have one egg or two between your legs."

"It's somewhat embarrassing to reveal this to you, but it's something you needed to know about me."

"It took much courage to tell me this. Not only did you earn a Purple Heart, but you should have one for bravery for revealing this to me," said Dark Cloud.

"Do you think Sarah would accept me like this?"

"When a woman wants a man, really wants a man, she'll take him as he is, missing a leg, an arm, or a whatever."

"I never thought of it that way. I guess I had tunnel vision on what I'd lost and not on what I still had." Tom smiled.

"A lot of people are like that. They focus on what they don't have rather than on what they do. See, that wasn't so hard, was it?" It took a moment for him to realize what he had said, but when he did, he said, "Sorry, no pun intended," and then Dark Cloud laughed.

Tom laughed too and said, "Yeah, guess that's about the long and short of it." When he realized his own faux pas, both he and Dark Cloud laughed heartily.

A horn honked, and Dark Cloud jerked the wheel sharply. "That was funny, but I better keep my eyes on the road. No point in either of us surviving war and then dying from careless driving."

"You got that right," said Tom. "People need us in one piece."

"The Great Provider has left us here for a reason. He's not done with us yet. There's still much to do before He calls us to be with Him."

They drove on down the highway toward the big city of Albuquerque. Whenever there was something of interest, Dark Cloud gave a running narrative to his passenger like a tour guide. He pointed to the black, and sharp volcanic rock area called the Malpais and the numerous Pueblo towns within sight of the road. "You can't see from here, but beyond those hills lie the Zuni people. Their language is unlike any other in the area. Some say it's similar to the Phoenicians from the Mediterranean Sea area. Don't ask me for an opinion 'cause I don't know. I do know about twelve miles to the south is the Acoma Reservation. You've seen the old village located high on a mesa. It's been in a bunch of Westerns. They claim it's the oldest constantly inhabited village in the Americas, but the Hopis will argue that point."

Tom mused over all this new information. There was a lot more history to this nation than he'd ever been taught in school. In less than an hour, they arrived at the airport. Tom got out and grabbed his Beatles suitcase. "You take good care of my hippie-mobile, yourself, and Sarah, okay?"

"I will, and you take good care of yourself, your father, and that suitcase. Sarah wants it returned in good condition."

"Not a problem. I want to thank you for arranging this flight and for all you've done for me while I was here. It still feels like a dream. I was so dreading coming here, and now I don't want to go. It seems like I have known you and Sarah forever."

"Roosevelt said during WWII, 'There's nothing to fear, but fear itself.' I've found that to be true most times, but a Jap with a machine gun is a fear I don't want to see again."

Tom nodded. “May we never see the horrors of war again.”

“I don’t think we will, but there are others in this world that relish killing and destruction,” said Dark Cloud. “They’ll have to be dealt with sometime in the future.”

“May our nation have strong men and women ready to meet the challenge.”

“Amen,” said Dark Cloud. “And now, I want to pray for you, Tom.” He looked a little sheepish but bowed his head. “Almighty God, Creator of all, keep this young man safe on the silver bird. Help him with what he needs when he reaches his home and bring him back to us in your timing. Amen.”

“Amen,” said Tom. “I’ll take care of myself, and you do the same.”

“I will, and you do the same too.” He reached forward and gave Tom a bear hug. Tom was surprised, but without shame, he hugged the older man back.

”Thank you for all you’ve done,” said Tom. “I’ve got to go, or I’ll miss my flight.” He could feel a tear welling up in his eye. He pulled away and started to walk toward the terminal. “Goodbye. I’ll see you again soon.”

“Hag’goo’nee’,” said Dark Cloud, “And Numbers 6:24-26.”

“What does that mean?”

“Goodbye, and if you don’t know the scripture, you need to look it up.”

“Thanks for everything,” said Tom.

“You, too. Have a safe flight.”

Tom headed to the building. Once inside, he looked out at his psychedelic microbus as it disappeared down the streets to Albuquerque. It was hard to believe he cared so much about two people he'd not even known a little over a week ago. *Dark Cloud got a long ride home. I wonder what I'll find at my home?*

Chapter 24

The next three months sped by quickly for Tom. He'd picked up how to drive the long bus in a New York minute. It wasn't too hard for a country boy who'd been operating farm tractors from the age of ten. The yellow Blue Bird bus wasn't much longer than some of their farm equipment. His father rode shotgun with him the first two days to help Tom learn the route, its stops, and the riders. He also pointed out the troublemakers, which came in handy.

Tom's dad's leg healed slowly, and by spring break, he was ready to take back the bus driver role. Tom made a point to call Sarah every other day. His dad complained about the long-distance billing on the phone, but Tom made a point of paying this and the whole bill. Things seem to be going well between them. Occasionally, he'd talk with Dark Cloud about conditions on the Big Rez. Two questions whispered in the back of his mind, and he finally got up the courage and asked. "Do I have your permission to ask for Sarah's hand? Do you think she'll come back to West Virginia to live?"

Dark Cloud readily said he was good with having Tom as a son-in-law, but as for the second question, Tom would have to ask Sarah, not him. Tom was happy with the answer to the first question but concerned about the second part. What if she said no? "No" to the marriage because she didn't want to leave the only home she'd ever known. He couldn't blame her. He knew how much he loved his home and wouldn't want to leave. Tom pondered on this and the possible outcomes. He knew how Caesar felt standing by the Rubicon River. Once crossed, there was no going back. He'd accept her decision either way and move on with or without her. On that same note, he'd put in job applications to local, large factories that always were hiring and applied to West Virginia University. He could use his GI Bill to pay for schooling if he needed it.

His father drove him to the airport in Baltimore for the noon flight back out west to Albuquerque. There he'd meet Dark Cloud, get his microbus back, and take care of unfinished matters on the Big Rez.

Part of the new Interstate Highway was complete, but not all of it. Someday, there'd be a four-lane limited-access road from Cumberland to Baltimore, but that was years away. Still, the road was much better than it was a few years ago when old, narrow, and winding US Route 40 went over every mountain between the two cities. Rumor had it that several miles of road going up Sideling Hill with its sweeping horseshoe turn on the top and then back down, would be replaced by making a deep cut through the mountain, but both men doubted they'd ever see it.

It was a clear day with a bright sun. Old Man Winter may still have a few tricks in his bag before he departed for good, but he was nowhere to be found that day. Perhaps he was saving it for an Easter finale. Some years, he went out like a lion.

Tom felt lucky to find a nonstop flight to Albuquerque. The three-hour flight took him directly over his home along Knobley Mountain in Mineral County, West Virginia. The plane was only half full, and Tom was able to pick the seat he wanted, one by the window. He loved to study and marvel at the landscape down below. A few years before Tom, his dad, and Wernher von Braun, the pilot of the three-person glider, flew over his home below, but today Tom was much higher and could see further. *Is this was how God saw the earth, so much smaller from His viewpoint, or did He see it even smaller as a little blue marble in His kaleidoscope of planets and galaxies?*

So much of what man saw as insurmountable problems must seem so tiny to the Creator of everything. Thinking about how big the whole universe was and how much bigger its Maker had to be, overwhelmed Tom's imagination. As he had heard a hippie say, "Man, it's mind-blowing."

The plane flew over the steep hills of Kentucky and the wide and muddy Mississippi River. He viewed the flat plains of Oklahoma and Texas with the vast green fields of winter wheat. Ahead, he saw the snow-covered Rocky Mountains. It was apparent why the songwriter had penned the words to the song, America the Beautiful.

The pilot announced that all should fasten seat belts and prepare for the upcoming landing. As the plane slowly descending, his ears popped. The aircraft flew over a gap where a long mountain dipped, and Tom felt it being buffeted by high winds forced upward by the mountain. It lasted only a few moments, and he was greatly relieved when it ended. The pilot banked the plane to the left toward the awaiting runway. The plane's wheels hit the pavement, bounced once, hit again, and stayed on the hardtop. The pilot reversed the engines and raised the flaps to slow the plane. They taxied to the terminal. The half-full plane quickly emptied. Tom had a large-sized carry-on bag and Sarah's small Beatles suitcase, so he didn't need to wait for any checked baggage.

Quickly, he found his way to the double doors into the arrival waiting area, and he saw Dark Cloud. Tom went over to him, and the two embraced.

"It's so good to see you," said Tom. "It seems like it was just yesterday when I left. Where's Sarah?" Tom said as he scanned the nearby crowd. Apprehension was thick in his question.

"Yes, good to see you," said Dark Cloud. "Sarah sends her best. She had to work at the mission. She tried to get off, but the mission daycare was already short-handed. Seems everyone but her has picked up the bug the kids are sharing. She'll be eagerly awaiting us in Lukachukai, especially you." He took Tom by the arm. "Come. I've something to show you."

They walked out into the cold New Mexico afternoon to the nearby parking garage and took the elevator to the third floor. After getting out, they took a right into the open and vacant top floor. Right in front of them was a VW microbus. He looked at Dark Cloud questioningly. Dark Cloud nodded, "Yup, that's your VW you left with me. That's the work of a guy on the Rez. He said he had always wanted to show he could do this, but never had the opportunity."

"It's beautiful." He walked around the van. "Who are all these guys?" He pointed to the incredible portraits painted where the psychedelic drawings were.

Dark Cloud said, "Some are local favorites. That's Sitting Bull in front of you. To his left is Crazy Horse. Next to him is Geronimo, and the next is Tuba."

"Tuba?"

"A great Navajo chief few people even in my tribe know of," Dark Cloud said. "So few remember the old ways and people, and I fear it will get worse unless we do something soon."

Tom pointed to the next man, "And who's this?"

"Tecumseh, the Shawnee warrior who nearly succeeded in uniting the eastern Indians, but was betrayed by his own brother."

"I've heard of him. Union General William Tecumseh Sherman was named after him. He marched through the South in the Civil War, and some down there still haven't forgotten or forgiven."

"One and the same," Dark Cloud said. He pointed to the mural covering the front of the van. It was somewhat different than the others. This Indian didn't look like a warrior, but more like a scholar. He wore mixed white and Indian garb, had spectacles on his nose, a quill pen and paper by his side, and smoked a long clay pipe. It had eastern tree species in the foreground and redwoods behind them. "Do you know who that is?"

"He looks familiar, but I don't know. Who is he?"

The older man smiled. "That's the great Cherokee man, Sequoia, first Indian to create an alphabet for his native language. The tallest trees in the world are named after him."

"Yeah, I thought the trees looked familiar. I saw them in California when I was there, but never put two and two together." He stopped and let out a whistle. "Man, this is a beautiful work of art. I wanted to get rid of the hippie painting, but wow, its over the top. How can I ever repay you?"

"It's all been taken care of. The artist is a young guy, Tonto Yazzi. Everyone said he was good. He overheard me talking at the Chapter House about wanting to get the van repainted for you, and he offered to do it for free. I asked him why he'd do it free gratis, and he said there was a catch. He had an appointment with the scholarship committee at Dine' College, and they wanted to see some of his work. He thought they'd be impressed with his paintings on your vehicle. They were overwhelmed when they saw them. The committee gave him a full scholarship, and you got a beautiful, painted van at no cost."

"That's fantastic. Not only will I walk in beauty, but I'll drive in beauty."

Dark Cloud tossed Tom the keys. "You drive for a while. I've already driven for five hours. You hungry?"

"Yeah, that Blake's place was pretty good. Is there one nearby?"

"Yeah, not far from here on Route 66."

"Good, and I should have stopped at the restroom at the airport. My eyes are starting to float."

Dark Cloud chuckled. "It's not far."

"Good," said Tom, "and my stomach's running on empty, too. Airline food's limited and what there is, leaves much to be desired."

"Then let's get going."

Tom placed his bags in the back of the van, which he noticed was spotless. Tom got in the microbus and started it. Dark Cloud gave him directions to Route 66, and a few minutes later, they were at Blake's. The parking lot was near full, and Tom found a spot under a gnarly old cottonwood tree. The men got out, walked into the restaurant, and headed straight to the bathroom. Much relieved, they washed their hands, exited the men's room, and got in the food line. When it was their turn, Dark Cloud ordered a cheeseburger with green chiles, fries, and a Coke. Tom told the cashier to make his the same. The cashier gave Tom a number, and they found a small table in the corner. A few minutes later, a young Indian woman in a Blake's shirt, brought them their order.

Dark Cloud blessed the meal and thanked the Lord for traveling mercies thus far and for the rest of the way home. After two quick "amens," the hungry men chowed down on the meals. Tom said, "This is good. I think I could get used to some of your Western food."

Dark Cloud said, "You got lots to learn about the food out here." They finished quickly and were soon back on Route 66 heading west. With Tom at the wheel, the city of Albuquerque disappeared behind them.

They made small talk on how the trip to Albuquerque had been for them, and what they'd been doing since they parted. After a moment of silence, Dark Cloud spoke, "I told her."

"You told her what?"

"I told her about your injury. She was a little surprised at first, but she made this comment, 'Glad that's all he lost. Many lost a whole lot more.' I think she was thinking of Chris when she said that."

Tom nodded, "I think she was, too. When you put it that way, it seems I've got a lot to be thankful for."

"You do. The Great Spirit decides the number of our days. He's not done with you, Tom. You need to make the most of what you've been given, and the first thing you need to do is to get your life right with Him, and then as we Navajo say, 'Walk in Beauty.'"

"That's some heavy-duty words, Dark Cloud."

"They are, but also very simple to do."

Tom said nothing more, and he caught Dark Cloud looking out the corner of his eye, probing Tom for his reaction. Tom remained silent and thought about what Dark Cloud said. They rode through the desert in silence on the new highway. Tom noticed his passenger's head starting to nod, and several minutes later, he was in dreamland and snoring.

Driving over here must have worn him out. Wonder what else he's been up to while I was gone? Dark Cloud stirred a little in his sleep, but soon was snoring again. Tom drove on, and the road reverted to the old two lane highway. He came to an intersection in

Gallup and made a right. At first, it didn't look right, but the number on the road sign was the one he remembered. As they approached Window Rock, Dark Cloud woke up. He stretched and asked, "Where are we? Guess I nodded off."

"I did, too," said Tom.

"That's not funny."

Tom smirked. "And you talked in your sleep about all your girlfriends on the Big Rez."

"Now, I'm sure I'm being played for a fool."

"Busted."

"Tom, you had me going for a while, but the truth is, I do have a lady friend on the Rez. Her name's Mai Ketsoh. Mai means Bright Flower, and I met her shortly after you left. I'd seen her at our little church, but did not know her but by sight. She showed up one day at the Chapter House looking for some help for her son. He got in some trouble down Flagstaff way, so I gave her the best information I could along with a couple of phone numbers for legal aid. She came back about two weeks later with good news about her son. Lawyer got him off on a legal point, and when he got back on the Rez, she boxed his head and read him the riot act. I think we'd had a lot less trouble here if parents would put the fear of the law and God Almighty into them, plus a few boots to the rear. I can't tell you how many I've seen get into a little trouble and just keep sinking deeper when the family didn't help or intervene. It's sad." He stopped and looked at Tom. "Sorry to burden you with that last part, but it's a grim reality here on the Rez. So, yeah, it's getting serious. We've been talking of getting married, soon."

Surprise showed on Tom's face. "You sly old dog. Looks like you've been very busy while I was gone. I hope it works out for you."

"Yes, I took Chris's death pretty hard, and it's about time the sun starts shining down on me." He looked to the right, and then back at Tom. "You missed the turnoff. We were talking, and I forgot to mention it."

Tom drove a little further until he found a convenient place to turn around. He stopped at the light and made a U-turn. They were back on the road to Lukachukai. He asked his passenger, "Did you have a restful nap?"

"Yeah, I did."

"Good. I'm getting tired, and I could use a snap, better known as a short nap. I'll pull over at that wide shoulder ahead, and you drive for a while, okay?"

"Will do. I thought you were looking tired. I'll take it from here."

Tom pulled over, and the two men changed places. Dark Cloud had them back on the road in a jiffy. Tom got comfortable and was soon asleep. Mile after mile passed when suddenly, Dark Cloud jerked the wheel of the van to the left and then to the right. Tom woke with a start. "What was that?"

"Coyote," said Dark Cloud, "and a dumb one at that. Nearly got run over."

"Was he chasing a roadrunner?"

"Didn't see one, but he did have a box under his arm that read, Acme something or the other. Coyote is a favorite character in Navajo stories."

"I'd like to hear the tales about them and not hit one."

Dark Cloud said, "Why don't you go back to sleep, and I'll be on the lookout for critters and anything else that we may encounter?"

"Like UFOs?"

"Roswell's in New Mexico. Only the lost ones show up here, and that's rare. Go back to sleep."

"Excellent idea," said Tom, and he was soon back sawing logs.

Dark Cloud looked over at his sleeping passenger. *Oh, to be young again. I wish I could be his age once more and know what I know now. Why do we get old so quick and smart so late?*

The long, empty miles ticked away one by one until they came to the little Indian town of Lukachukai. Dark Cloud swung a hard right from the main road to Buffalo Pass Road running through the town. In about a half-minute, he turned onto a side street, and in less than a block was at his home. Dark Cloud had no sooner turned off the air-cooled engine when Sarah burst out of the house. Tom opened his door, and Sarah practically leaped at him. She gave him a bear hug and a long kiss. He was more than happy to do his part in this exercise.

"I've missed you so," she said.

"If I'd known I'd be getting this kind of a greeting, I'd have tried to return sooner." Their lips met again and parted after a lengthy kiss.

Tom said, "I missed you, too."

Dark Cloud cleared his throat. "Okay, you two lovebirds may have your love to keep you warm, but this old guy is getting cold. Get inside the house. I know Sarah has coffee and warm food waiting for us. Ain't that right, Sarah?"

The two lovers and Dark Cloud went inside of the welcoming house. After a great, hot meal, they sat around the table, catching up on time apart. Tom helped Sarah clean the table and wash the dishes. Dark Cloud sat in his big, overstuffed chair and read *The Navajo Times*. Though his eyes were on the paper, his ears were listening to the friendly small talk between the two. He could see where this was going, and he had no problem with it. Perhaps, if things went as he thought they would, he should move up his plans.

Dark Cloud yawned and said, "I'm tired from the long drive. I'm going to bed. Good night. I'll see you in the morning." Tom and Sarah talked for a while longer, but once their lips met, the two behaved like long lost lovebirds that had found each other again. They found it hard to tear themselves apart from one another, but somehow they did. Sarah went to her room for the night, and Tom lay down on the hide-a-bed in the great room, thinking. Although he was tired, his mind remained clear, and he knew what he'd do tomorrow. He heard the sounds of two sleeping people coming from the nearby rooms, and soon he added his own sounds to the chorus. Tomorrow was another day, and all three would need a restful night for everything to go well.

Chapter 25

Tom stirred in his sleep. Something pleasant tickled his nose, the smell of bacon. He opened his eyes and looked around the great room from the sofa bed where he lies. The table in the far side of the room was set for breakfast, Sarah was cooking at the stove. How she had managed to achieve all of this, he didn't know. She had her back to him as she concentrated on her work. "Good morning to you."

A little startled, she turned to him and said, "You surprised me. I was trying to get this done before you two guys awoke."

Tom sat up in the bed, "I believe you'd have gotten it all done, but the smell of the bacon betrayed you. I'm surprised you achieved as much as you did without awakening me. Opening cabinets and shuffling plates, glasses, and silverware usually make plenty of noise. Either you were quiet as a mouse, or I was dead tired."

She smiled, "Maybe a little of both."

"I think you are right. Give me a minute, and I'll help you." He slid out of the hide-a-bed and put on his jeans. Then, he folded the bed up into a couch. He walked past her to the bathroom. "Nature calls."

She laughed, "Hope everything comes out okay."

He smiled at her as he closed the bathroom door. After taking care of business and freshened himself up, he went back to the kitchen and helped Sarah finish the meal. A cup of coffee was waiting for him, and he was more than grateful to see it. He took a sip. *A little bitter. Some of yesterday's brew. Navajos could give hillbillies some lessons on how to be frugal.*

Tom heard Dark Cloud stirring in his bedroom. Shortly afterward, he appeared dressed but sleepy-eyed and headed for the bathroom without saying much more than "Hello."

He spent a few minutes in the bathroom while Tom and Sarah placed food on the plates. Dark Cloud came out, looked at the table, and said, "I like this. Sarah, we should have company more often." She smiled but said nothing. The three sat at the table, and Dark Cloud said, "Hope this coffee is strong. I was doing too much thinking last night. Didn't go to sleep till after midnight and will need this to keep alert today. A lot of important things will happen today; I know it."

They made small talk over breakfast. Tom asked about the road over Buffalo Pass. Dark Cloud told him it was best traveled by 4-wheel drive vehicles now. A few 2-wheel drives had made it over, but the snow on the road would discourage all but fools and the brave and adventurous, and sometimes it was hard to tell the difference. His advice was not to attempt it if he was thinking of trying.

They finished the meal along with the pot of strong coffee. Dark Cloud said he had something to do over at the Chapter House, and he soon left. Tom and Sarah cleaned the table and washed the few dishes used for the meal.

Tom suggested a short drive with Sarah, and soon they were in the VW microbus and heading toward Buffalo Pass. She asked, "You're not thinking of going to that special place where we were before on the east side of the mountain after what my dad told you, are you?"

"I'd like to go there, but with the road being as it is, no, we aren't going there, but someplace much closer."

Sarah was silent for a moment and then spoke, "It sure is cold in here. Is the heater on?"

"Yeah, it's on, but these air-cooled machines just don't produce heat like a water-cooled engine does. If there's one thing I could change on this van, it would be how it heats. The mileage is great, and it works really well for camping and fun stuff like that, but the heater leaves something to be desired."

"You can say that again. It can't be much warmer in here than outside."

Tom said, "It takes a while to get perking, and I don't think it will get hot before we reach our destination." At that moment, he turned the right turn signal on, traveled a few hundred feet, and then onto the dirt road that led to the village overlook.

"I thought this might be where we were going. I wanted to come here." Her comment surprised him.

The frozen ground crunched under the wheels. A little snow remained in places protected from the sun. It didn't take long for them to reach the parking spot at the end of the road and stop there. Quickly, Sarah was out of the van ahead of Tom. He followed her to the overlook at the cliff's edge. Early morning sun rays fell on the small Indian town.

"Lukachukai," she said. "It ain't much, but it's home."

"Sounds like where I come from. I've now seen a bunch of the world, but home will always be where I grew up." He was silent for a minute and then asked, "Have you ever thought of leaving here?"

"I've been thinking a lot about that recently. I'm eighteen, and I've wondered what I should do with my life. I like working at the mission, but at times, I have this wanderlust in me. I've seen people live their whole lives here, never going more than 50 miles from where they were born. Some seem happy to do so, but others have a sad look like they wished they'd done something different, but now it's too late."

A cold winter breeze blew Sarah's hair around, at least the part that was out of the parka with the big hoodie. Tom took her glove-covered hand in his and said, "Look, ah, I, ah, really don't know how they do it here on the reservation. Things seem so much in flux. One never knows if we're in the white man's world, the Indian world, or some combination of the two, so I'm just going to ask you the best I can."

She looks a little surprised but smiled playfully. "Okay, confused man, what do you want to know?"

He swallowed. "It's a two-part question, and I need you to answer both parts. Will you come live with me in West Virginia," he paused, "and will you be my wife? Sarah, I was in love with you the first day I met you. I can understand if you said no to either part."

"Yes, and yes," she said.

"I know it's asking a lot from you. You'd have to leave all you know and come live with a guy you just met."

"Tom, my answers are yes and yes." She smiled at the dumbfounded Tom.

"You did say yes and yes, right?" Her face was a broad smile. She nodded."You said yes and yes." Slowly, her answers sand into Tom's thick skull. He smiled broadly and grabbed both her hands. "You said yes and yes." She nodded again. He threw his arms around her, and she him. They looked eye-to-eye.

She said, "I said yes and yes." Their lips met, and the cold around them vanished from the heat of their long kiss that could melt the sun. Tom dropped his hands to Sarah's. He turned to the sleepy town far off and yelled, "Hey, Lukachukai. She said yes and yes." He dropped his hand from hers and turned to the east. He put his hands to his mouth and yelled, "Hey, Big R, she said yes and yes." He turned once more and yelled at no one in particular, "Hey, world, she said yes and yes," and then he hugged her again.

She smiled at him. "Tom, I think I made you happy, and I think you let everyone on this planet know."

"I'm so happy, and to think, I never knew you a few months ago. It's strange how events work out. To think if I'd never met Chris…"

Sarah said, "I know he'd be happy for us. He mentioned you in a letter he sent from Vietnam. He said he'd met a guy, another soldier, who he wished that somehow, somewhere, this Tom fellow could meet me. I think he got his wish."

Tom said, "There's an old Jewish proverb that goes something like this, 'Out of evil, a little good can come. Out of destruction, rebirth can happen.' We can't change what happened in the past, but we can build on it for the future."

"I was so hoping you'd ask me for my hand. I thought you'd ask me to come with you, but it was the second question I prayed the most about. I asked Dark Cloud for advice on this. He's a good man full of wisdom, real wisdom, not the foolishness of this world that passes for wisdom. There was a tear in his eye when he answered me. He said two things I shall never forget, 'Follow beauty wherever it takes you, and follow your heart.' And I shall do both with you, Tom."

Tom smiled and thought of how different but how similar his father and her father were. Still waters run deep.

She took his hand and led him to a large, flat, and smooth red rock where they sat down side-by-side touching. Tom said, "I had all these things to say if you answered no to either question, and you made me the happiest, but most dumbfounded man alive when you said yes to both questions. I'm the luckiest man alive."

"Tom, you knucklehead, do yourself a favor. Hush up and kiss me."

He placed his arms around her and gladly did as told. It was a long kiss, again. When their lips parted, they held each other tightly and gazed off toward the town below. Neither said much as the reality of what they'd done sank in. The couple sat another ten minutes enjoying each other's company. A breeze picked up, and Tom pulled his collar up tighter. "As much as I'm enjoying this, the wind's starting to cut into me here on this exposed rock."

"I know," said Sarah. "When the sun warms things up, the wind gets to going. It seems like it's always windy in this desert. Will West Virginia be like that?"

"No. It gets cold like here, but it can be damp and rainy, and the wind doesn't blow all the time. Sometimes in the summer, when it's so hot and sticky, you wish you could buy a breeze, but you can't no matter how much money you have. What do you say we get off this cold rock, head back to town, and tell the folks what we've done?"

"Sounds good to me." They hopped off the rock and headed toward the vehicle holding hands. Tom fired the van up, and they headed back down the frozen lane. He took a left on the paved road and drove toward the town. The sun hit the large, red rocks which lined the canyon and made its different shades shine.

What a beautiful place. Tom mouthed something Dark Cloud had said, "May beauty surround you."

"What did you say?" asked Sarah.

"Oh, sorry, just thinking out loud. It was something your father said, 'May beauty surround you.'"

"It's a stark beauty, and I'll miss it."

"I will too, but I believe you'll soon learn to love the green tree-covered hills of Appalachia."

She smiled, "I think I will, and with you by my side, we can face the world."

"We will, but first, we face your dad. How do you think he'll take the news?"

"Only one way to know for sure. I think he's been expecting it. Wonder what his big plans he mentioned are?"

"Can't be any more of a surprise than we've got for him," Tom said.

Chapter 26

"Saturday?" exclaimed Tom and Sarah. "Saturday?"

"Yes, this Saturday coming," Dark Cloud. said, "It has to be this Saturday."

"Why so soon? Can't we have a little more time to prepare for this?" pleaded Sarah. "There's so much to do to prepare for a wedding."

"Yeah, I know. I saw the look in your eyes, and I figured I'd better do some checking on available buildings for a wedding and people to marry you," said Dark Cloud. "The only place open now while they are refurbishing the mission chapel is the big room at the Chapter House. And the only open date for months is this Saturday. The church's booked all the events that usually occur at the chapel in the Chapter House for the next several months. It's either now, or months off. You should thank me for the foresight and looking for you."

Sarah's face fell. "Dad, do you really think we can pull it all together by next Saturday?"

"I do, but I know we'll be busy, and we won't need any big surprises. I checked at the trading post, and they've suits for men and beautiful, traditional dresses for you. They can prepare some of the food and the ladies auxiliary; I know, can produce a meal fit for a chief or a wedding reception with little notice and be happy to do it. And, at a reasonable price. We can do it," he assured her.

"I thought we'd have more time."

Dark Cloud smiled. "By tomorrow night, everyone on the Big Rez will know about your wedding. News of this nature travels like wildfire on the moccasin telegraph. Tom, it's kind of like the white man's, heard it through the grapevine, only we use smoke signals."

Sarah rolled her eyes, "Daddy."

"Oh, all right. We'll spread the news with the telephone. And one more thing. You know traditionally, the Dine' have very little time between an agreement of marriage and the wedding, and it's one tradition I want to keep, plus it gives the couple less time to get cold feet."

Sarah said nothing and seemed to be thinking. She looked at Tom and asked, "What do you think?"

Tom was thinking about all this, and now was the moment to voice an opinion. He wanted to crawl under a rug and hide, but that wasn't an option. He smiled his best smile and said, "Sarah, if tradition says it should be, and your father says we can do it, let's do it. The thought of having you as my wife and returning home with you sooner than later sounds much better to me."

Dark Cloud's smile flattened out when he heard of their decision to leave, but he forced a smile. "Sarah, I want you to be happy and with your husband. I knew you might be leaving, but it just hit me on what it will be like not seeing you every day." He paused and sniffled through his nose. "Honey, I love you and want nothing, but the best for you today and forever."

Sarah hugged her dad and said, "I know you do. You always have, ever since I can remember." Tears ran from her eyes.

Tom went to them, and it became a group hug. When it ended, Tom asked, "Well, what do we do first?"

Dark Cloud looked at him like he was silly and said, "How about we have lunch before we go over our plan of attack? You know an army, white or Indian, travels on its stomach."

Tom and Sarah laughed at his little joke. The trio got some sandwich material from the small refrigerator and a large can of soup off of the shelf. Lunch was ready in a jiffy. There was much to do, and a short time to get it done.

***

Over the next few days, it was rush, rush, rush for the all involved. As father of the bride, Dark Cloud made a point of running the whole operation. The ladies' auxiliary decorated the Chapter House and made plans for the food needed - items. Dark Cloud took Tom to the trading post, and they were both measured for new, dressy, blue jeans, a long-sleeve white shirt, a sky blue dress jacket, and new black boots. Tom needed a new belt, so Dark Cloud helped him pick out one with a large silver buckle and lots of turquoise and decorations. A traditional turquoise necklace and a purple headband would finish out their garb. "Guys have it easy," Tom told Dark Cloud, who agreed. The older man told Tom that Mai, his lady friend, was helping Sarah pick out her bridal dress and accessories. Dark Cloud and Mai would be their witnesses at the wedding. Neither man was to see the ladies' outfits until the wedding. It would be the one surprise, planned of course, for the big day. All seemed to be on track. What could go wrong?

***

Thursday evening, supper time

Tom sat on the old couch, his bed for the last week. He'd read several small books he'd found at the Charter House lending library about the Navajo people and their legends. They were mainly children's books on the story of creation, how they won their freedom after the forced removal from Dine'tah and their return, and of course, many tales of the antics of Coyote, the trickster. He seems always to be getting into trouble with a ruse that often backfired on him. Tom wondered if perhaps this was where Warner Brothers got their idea for the Road Runner and Coyote cartoons. Perhaps. Sarah sat at the other end of the couch, reading with her feet and legs pulled up in front of her. Her book was one about the Sackett family called *The Daybreakers* by Louis L'Amour. Tom was surprised at how popular the author was on the reservation. Someone had donated at least a dozen to the library, and from the wear on the pages, this one was well-read long before Sarah got the copy. He eyed at her inviting form and thought of the delights awaiting them on the honeymoon. They'd take their time traveling back to West Virginia and see whatever sights were on the way, whichever way they chose on the journey. A sly smile came to his face. At that time, Sarah glanced up and saw Tom looking at her. "What?" she asked. He smiled more and she asked again, "What?" She realized what he was thinking. "Oh," she said and smiled broadly as did Tom. Dark Cloud seemed not to notice. He was absorbed in an article in *The Navajo Times* newspaper.

Tom took his mind off of the pleasures ahead and stuck his nose back in his book. A few minutes later, that same nose told him the lamb stew cooking on the stove would soon be ready. His eyes fell on the table. *Odd, Dark Cloud set the table for four, not the three that are here. Guess we'll have company, but who? He hasn't mentioned anything about a guest sharing the meal. Whatever he is up to will be revealed soon.*

Tom read a few more pages in the Coyote storybook. Coyote was hungry decided to satisfy his appetite with his cousin, Horned Toad. He swallowed him whole and thought how smart and clever he was. His pleasure soon turned to horror when Horned Toad began to move around and poke Coyote's insides. He begged Horned Toad to leave, but he said it was nice and warm inside, and he liked it there. He didn't want to leave. Coyote tried desperate measures like beating himself and swallowing a river of water to drown Horned Toad, but still, he wouldn't go. Finally, Coyote pleaded with Horned Toad to leave. He said he would if Coyote apologized and promised never to do it again. He gladly did and Horned Toad left. Coyote realized he'd not been wise, but a fool. A wise Coyote didn't make hasty decisions but would think his plan through. Tom could imagine old Navajo grandfathers telling their grandchildren Coyote and similar native tales as lessons about life.

A knock at the door brought Dark Cloud to his fee. "Now, who can that be?"

Tom had his suspicions that Dark Cloud already knew the answer to his rhetorical question. As Sherlock Holmes said, "*Surely, the game is afoot.*"

The door opened, and a woman walked in, greeted Dark Cloud with a kiss, and exchanged hugs and salutations with the younger folk.

Dark Cloud said, "Tom, this is Mai, my lady friend. I invited her tonight so we could get to know each other better."

Mai gave Dark Cloud her coat. He took it into the bedroom and quickly returned. "I think supper should be ready. Let's eat, and then we'll chitchat."

They all pitched in and had the food on a table in a jiffy. After a short blessing by Dark Cloud, they had a delightful meal mixed with small talk and some specific information on details of the upcoming wedding.

Tom had the feeling something was up, so he got their attention and said, "I've had the feeling that this meeting's more than just a happy meal among friends. I know it's presumptuous, but I think you two," he pointed to Dark Cloud and Mai, "are holding something back."

The older couple grinned. Dark Cloud spoke, "We are. Guess some things are hard to hide. I'd been thinking of asking Mai for her hand for some time, and when you and Sarah decided to get married, I asked Mai to marry me, and she said yes."

"Daddy, I'm so happy for you. I was worried about you all alone, and now I know you won't be." She got up from the table and hugged the seated couple. "It's an answer to prayers."

"We have one more surprise for you," Dark Cloud said.

"Thought you were the one who wanted no surprises," Tom said.

Dark Cloud smiled, "I hope this is a pleasant and agreeable surprise. We'd like to make it a double wedding and also for you two to be our witnesses. What do you say?"

Tom looked at Sarah, and her eyes said yes. He knew if it was okay with her, it was okay with him. He'd not go against the wishes of the bride. All eyes were on him, and he said, "Okay." The three across the table exploded with joy, and they forgot about Tom. For that moment, time seemed suspended for him. *If anyone a year ago had told me how my life would go in the coming year, I'd said they were bonkers. Meet a wild and crazy guy named Johnnie, get in trouble, end up in the Army, go to Vietnam, nearly get killed, almost not keep a promise I made to a dying man, meet Chris' father and sister who in a few days would be my family, and now, also have a new mother-in-law or whatever they're called in the matriarchal Navajo way of thinking that I understand so little of, I'd said they're delusional or writing a soap opera.* But here he was, and somehow he knew this was exactly where he was supposed to be. He couldn't explain it, but in his heart, he knew it was so. *Wonder what the Writer of this story has in mind for Sarah and me in the next year?*

Chapter 27

The day of the wedding couldn't arrive soon enough for Tom, and he could see the others also were eager for the big day to come. Dark Cloud explained to Tom how the wedding, a mix of traditional and modern, would go. Tom hoped he'd remember it all, but Dark Cloud told him if he forgot, follow his example, and everything would go smoothly. He hoped the older man was right. The short rehearsal the day before went reasonably smooth.

On the night before the wedding, Sarah went to stay at Mai's home. Dark Cloud told him it was bad luck to see the bride or brides. Tom had a hard time falling asleep that night as did Dark Cloud, but after a while, Tom heard him snoring. He wondered about the wisdom of marrying this young woman whom he'd only known for a few short months. She was from the western USA and he, the East. They were both part Indian but different tribes. She'd consented to come with him, but was it fair to her, her father, and her friends on the reservation? Would the people around the Cumberland area accept her? *So many unanswered questions.* The only thing he was sure of was he wanted Sarah as his wife, and they'd sort out the other issues the best they could as they came up. Life was like that. Smooth as silk and predictable from day-to-day until an unseen hand throws a monkey wrench in the gears, and life's never the same again.

Tom woke the next morning to the smell of coffee brewing and bacon frying. He looked at the table and saw four hard-boiled eggs with steam rising from them in a clear bowl placed in the center. He rolled out of bed and put his pants to put on.

"Good morning, Tom. I trust you slept well," Dark Cloud said.

"I had a little trouble getting' to sleep. You went down before I did."

"I remember the feeling - cold feet and jitters. I think every groom has them, especially the first time around. Do what you have to in the bathroom, and I'll have breakfast ready to eat by the time you're done."

"You've taken care of everything."

"I try to. Don't like surprises."

Tom smiled, walked into the bathroom, and closed the door. When he was done and freshened up, he walked to the table and sat down. Dark Cloud had two plates set out with toast, two eggs, and bacon and a large cup of hot coffee next to it. "This looks great. Is this the traditional Navajo breakfast you serve before a wedding?"

"No, a funeral."

Tom was surprised. Dark Cloud said, "Just kidding, my attempt at some gallows humor. It's the end of our bachelor days. We're kinda like dead men walking."

"What?"

"I'm pulling your leg. Just nervous and wanting this done and over." Tom nodded in agreement. Dark Cloud continued, "This isn't a wedding meal. You'll get the traditional cornmeal there." He paused. "The eggs say I want you and Sarah to make many babies. I need a bunch of grandchildren to spoil."

Tom shifted uneasily at the thought of his soon to be father-in-law's reference to sex, so he decided to press his luck."Okay, I can see why you gave me eggs, but what about you? Why do you have eggs?"

Dark Cloud grinned, "You never know. This old dog still has fire in the furnace, and you never know."

They laughed. After eating the late breakfast and cleaning up, the men went to the closet, got out their wedding attire, and quickly put them on.

"How do I look?" asked Tom.

"Like a lamb going to sacrifice."

"You do too."

"I know," said the older man. "Goodbye freedom. We better get going. If we're late, I don't think the old excuse about being on Indian time will do today."

They left the house and walked the short distance to the Chapter House. Inside, they found a lot of people already there. The room was joyfully decorated with a mixture of Anglo and Navajo décor for the wedding. They mingled with the well-wishers. Two men, the local priest and a Navajo elder, who'd both officiate the ceremony, approached them and gave last-minute instructions. The two grooms were to stand in front by them, and then the brides would walk up the aisle side-by-side. Once in front, they would stand beside their appropriate groom.

The two men greeted guests for a few more minutes until the ceremony began. Four young men chanted as they drummed. Tom seemed puzzled. Dark Cloud saw this and said, "They're giving traditional blessings for the wedding. I see they want us up in the front with the priests. Let's go."

The two men went to the front with the mission priest and the Navajo elder, a pastor from the local church. Once there, the drumming and chanting dropped in volume and then stopped. The drummers remained seated and turned to the rear of the building as all did. A white woman whom Tom had never seen before began to play the traditional music of "Here Comes the Bride" on a piano. From a doorway in the back, the two brides emerged. Both Tom and Dark Cloud smiled. The two women were beautifully dressed alike. They wore a brightly toned cap of several colors covered with strings of beads also of many colors. Their brown dresses went to mid-calf and had fringes on the sleeves and at the bottom. Both women's hair was braided and had pretty ribbons on the braids. Large turquoise earrings dangled from Mai's ears. Sarah's were somewhat smaller. Both wore necklaces of black, brown, and an almost transparent stone of some sort. Their shin coverings reminded Tom of the leg guards a baseball catcher wore, but these were multicolored turquoise, red, and white patterns. The brown moccasins also had many braids of similar hues.

The music played as the two women made their way to the front to their awaiting grooms. They stood next to them, and the four were all smiles.

The Navajo elder spoke,

"Now, you will feel no rain, for you will be shelter for each other."

"Now, you will feel no cold, for each of you will be warmth to the other."

"Now, there is no more loneliness, for each of you will be a companion to the other."

"Now, you are two bodies, but there is only one life before you."

"Soon, you will go to your resting place, to enter into the days of your togetherness."

"May your days be good and long upon the earth."

Then the priest spoke,

"Above you are the stars, and below you are the stones."

"As time does pass, remember;"

"Like a star, should your love be constant."

"Like a stone should your love be firm."

"Be close, yet not too close."

"Possess one another, yet be understanding."

"Have patience with the other; for storms will come, but they will go quickly."

"Be free in giving of affection and warmth."

"Make love often, and be sensuous to one another."

"Have no fear, and let not the ways of words of the unenlightened give you unease."

"For the Great Spirit, our Lord, is with you, now and always."

The Navajo pastor asked the people there, "Who would like to give these couples advice and wisdom they'll need for their lives together?"

Over the next ten minutes, mainly men, but a few women spoke to the couples. Some spoke in Navajo, some in English, and some freely went from one language to the other. Most of the advice was meaningful, but some were funny. One elderly woman with skin like leather and spoke only in Navajo, had everyone laughing except the priest who blushed. Tom asked Sarah, "What did she say that got that reaction?"

Sarah smiled awkwardly and whispered, "She was telling us what she thought was the best position for us to make a boy baby."

"Oh." He grinned, as did Sarah.

Several more people spoke, but none created the commotion like the old woman had. When it was apparent all who wanted to talk had, the Navajo pastor and the priest instructed the two couples to come forward. They extended their hands, and he poured water from a vase with two openings at the top and black and brown patterns on the side. The priest spoke to the crowd, "This symbolizes purity and cleansing." Several heads nodded. Next, the Navajo elder and the priest took a bowl each and poured white and yellow corn pollen into them, added a little water to make mush. He said, "The male white pollen and the female yellow pollen are mixed, and the two are now one." He then ran his finger from left to right through the middle of the mush pie and next from top to bottom. "This is for the four sacred mountains that make up the corners of Dine'tah. Now, eat from all four parts and then the center."

The men went first, starting in the east where the morning began, and the women followed their example. They went clockwise to all four parts and the center lastly. The priest spoke, "This also represents the four stages in life: birth, youth, maturity, and death. May you live long and remain in love forever." The priest and pastor took the bowl of corn pollen to the people who took a pinch with their fingers and passed it on.

In unison, the priest and pastor instructed the couple in front of them, "Repeat after me, 'I, (say your name) take you (say your spouse's name) as my (wife or husband)." The priest paused as they began reciting after him. "I do solemnly avow my love for you. I will comfort you, keep you, love you, and defend you in sickness or in health, in riches or poverty, in sorrow or joy, seeking only to be with you until death parts us. All these things I pledge upon my honor.'

"Now, we bless the rings. Place them on your new spouse's finger as we speak, 'Circles have no beginning and have no end, and so in the long and sacred tradition of marriage, rings have come to symbolize eternal love and the endless union of body, of mind, and of the spirit Aho! This ring is a symbol of my love and faithfulness, and with all that I am, and all that I have, I honor you, and pledge to you my love and life.' Amen.

"Now, as you have consented together in matrimony and have pledged your faith to each other by the giving and the receiving of these rings before your family and community, according to the powers invested in me by the State of Arizona and the Navajo Nation, I now pronounce you husband and wife."

The couples kissed, and the audience cheered. When the din had quieted, an old and honored man, Hosteen Chi, rose to his feet. All eyes were on him. He cleared his throat and began to speak, "You have lit a fire, and that fire should not go out. The two of you now have a fire that represents love, understanding and a philosophy of life. It will give you heat, food, warmth, and happiness. This new fire represents a new beginning - a new life and a new family. The fire should keep burning. You should stay together. You have lit the fire for life until old age separates you. Wake in beauty always."

The couples smiled and hugged. The priest and the pastor congratulated the couples and walked away, signaling the end of the ceremony. The crowd rushed forward and engulfed the newlyweds. The room filled with happy sounds. After about ten minutes of merrimaking, the couples went to the head of the food line and got a traditional lamb soup, fry bread, chocolate kisses, and a drink. Tom got some coffee. The crowd followed and did the same. Twenty minutes later, the couples opened their gifts. Some envelopes contained money. The boxes mainly contained household goods and clothing, some of it handmade. Tom opened one box and quietly put it to the side, closing it back up. Curious, Sarah asked, "What was it?"

"A box of prophylactics."

"We won't need them."

"There's always a joker in every deck." Sarah nodded and said no more about the incident.

After all the gifts were opened, and the crowd thinned, Dark Cloud approached Tom and Sarah. He said, "The ladies' auxiliary is taking care of all cleaning and tidying up, so the four of us are free to leave and…I have a surprise for you."

"I thought you didn't like surprises."

"I lied, but I think you'll like this one."

"What is it?"

"It will have to wait until we get to my house."

Chapter 28

Tom and Sarah changed clothes in her bedroom at the house she and her father, Dark Cloud, called home, but for Sarah, it would be the last time it would be home. She'd have a new one soon. "Sure going to miss this place. As I've said before, it ain't much, but it's home."

Tom hugged his new wife. "I think I can understand. When I left home for the Army, it felt like I'd never return. I had a big knot in my stomach."

"I have that knot too, but I have a honeymoon and a new husband to comfort the blow. You had boot camp and a growling drill instructor frothing at the mouth."

"Never thought of it that way. Still, it has to be hard to say goodbye to the only home you've ever known."

"I'll adjust with you," she said. "What do you think Dad's surprise is? It was as much a bolt out of the blue for me as it was for you."

"Guess we will know soon. I hear them coming out of your father's room now."

Tom and Sarah went into the living room. He said, "We put all the rented clothes in the plastic covers or boxes they came in. I'm dying with curiosity. What's the surprise?"

Dark Cloud said, “Thanks for taking care of the clothes. We did the same with ours. You’ll find the receipts and papers and need them when you return them tomorrow. They have to be in by noon.”

Tom was puzzled, and he looked at Sarah. She shrugged her shoulders and shook her head.

Dark Cloud spoke again, “I knew you were planning on spending your first night in the microbus. Well, I’m going to Mai’s house for the night so you can be alone here in this house. I thought it would be better. Charlie told me yesterday his snowplow broke down when he was clearing the way up to our favorite spot through Buffalo Pass on the mountain overlooking Shiprock. He got it fixed and is clearing the road now, but he isn’t done yet. He’ll have it done by tomorrow morn and seeing how you are going to be here then, and I thought you could return the clothes to the general store. Sound like a plan?”

“Sounds good to me,” said Tom.

“I like it. Thank you, Dad. You’re the best.”

“Good. Then, it’s settled. After you return the clothes, just head for the mountain. We’ll see you before you leave for good. Come on down after a couple of days, and we’ll be here,” said Dark Cloud. “We’ll be leaving now. See you in a few days.” With that, they grabbed their coats and left.

Tom put his arms around Sarah and said, “Mrs. Kenney. It has a nice sound to it.”

Sarah put her fingers to his lips to shut them, and then she kissed them.

After a long kiss, their lips parted. Tom said, “I think I like this.”

"Well, my husband, are you ready for the main course?"

Tom smiled and kissed her passionately. In a few short moments, they slipped into the bedroom and clothes went flying in all directions.

By now, Dark Cloud and Mai were nearly to her house. She looked at Dark Cloud, smiled, and asked, "Do you think they're naked by now?"

"Yup," he said.

"Well, what's keeping us?"

Dark Cloud raised his eyebrows and said, "Woman, I'm not a horny teenager anymore. Back seat won't do. Can you wait till we get to your house?"

"I can wait that long, but not a minute longer. Promise and hope to die?'

"I promise, but none of this dying stuff, okay?"

"If you do die, it'll be from exhaustion," she said with a big grin. And she was right.

Chapter 29

September 5, 1997, Afternoon on top of Knobley Mountain

Tom woke with a start. He looked toward the commotion that had awakened him. A small deer, a yearling, ran swiftly across the old mountain field. *Wonder what spooked him?* The answer came quickly as a coyote bounded out of the woods after the fleeing deer. Tom reached for the gun he'd brought with him, but before he got off a shot, the coyote and deer were gone. *Just as well. Still half asleep and don't think I had much chance of hitting him anyway.*

He rubbed his eyes. The intruders that interrupted the afternoon peace and his dream were gone like nothing had ever happened. *Darn coyotes. Getting to be so many of them. Wished I'd got that one. He's gone and won't be back.*

Peace returned to the old field. The sun was warm, and a slight breeze moved the pines nearby. *I must have been dreaming, but what was I dreaming about? I know the answer is there somewhere...Sarah. It seemed so real like it was yesterday. I loved her so.*

Tom let out a long sigh and lie back down on the pile of leaves. He pulled his hat down over his face and closed his eyes. *Oh, Sarah, how I loved you. Why did you have to go so soon?*

In a few short minutes, Tom's breath became shallow and slow, and he began to snore - back to dreamland.

October 22, 1966, Morgantown, WV

"I don't wanna go," Tom said. "I planned on staying right here in our apartment, having some lunch, and then walking over to the stadium for the game."

"But Tom, I told them I'd be there, and I'd like you to come, please," said Sarah. "They're such nice and friendly people, and we haven't made many friends while here. You've been so busy with classes and me working, seems we haven't done much together lately. You know I don't understand football, but I said I'd go with you to the game against Penn State. Will you do this for me?"

He knew he was in a losing battle, and she was right. They'd been busy and doing much together as a couple. She'd started going to a weekly Bible study at the assistant football coach's house, and Tom had heard all about how much she liked the people and what they were learning. Tom hadn't been able to figure out what a burly football coach would have to do with the Bible, and he was curious about this. "Okay," he said.

"Did I just hear you say you'd go?"

"Yeah, but under one condition."

"What's that?"

"Tomorrow, I get to watch my team play, and there'll be no interruptions."

"Deal," she said. "You can watch the Steamers play and no interruptions."

"Steelers," corrected Tom. "My team's the Pittsburgh Steelers. Blue and gold on Saturday and black and gold on Sunday. Go Steelers!"

"Okay, Mountaineers on Saturday and Steelers on Sunday. I won't forget. I'll remember. The hunchback's name is Nelsen, Bill Nelsen, right?"

Tom cringed and said, "You got the name right, but he's called a quarterback, not a hunchback."

" Hey, I'm trying."

"Yeah, I know you are. Guess girls didn't have much contact with football on the reservation."

"No," she said. "We didn't. I saw the boys play, but it didn't make much sense to me. Things here are so much different. It's going to take a while to get used to the trees and the seasons, green in the summer, then the many colors in the fall, and now all brown after the leaves have fallen."

"Things are different here, but people wherever you go, seem about the same."

"Yeah," she said. "I've noticed that. You knew what surprised me during the Bible study? I noticed how people who lived a thousand or more years ago had the same hopes, dreams, wants, and failures as people today."

"That's interesting," said Tom. "When's the pre-game get-together again?"

"We need to leave about now."

"Okay," he said. "I'll be ready."

Tom grabbed his heavy sweatshirt, the one with WVU Mountaineers printed on the front and a windbreaker. There'd been some frost a week before, but this week, it was Indian summer. Sarah had been puzzled about this, but Tom's explanation satisfied her. He told her the expression went back to colonial days. It described a time in the fall when the air was unusually warm and dry.

Sarah went into the small bathroom of the third-floor attic apartment and closed the door. He could hear her scurrying around. *Women. Don't know if I'll ever understand them. They say let's go, and then you wait ten minutes for them to get everything ready to go. When a man says, let's go, he's ready to go.*

Ten minutes later, she came out. "Now, let's go. I look much better, don't I?"

To Tom, she looked pretty much the same, but only a dummy would say that, so, he said, "You look great, honey. I love you." Sometimes truth could get a man in the doghouse, and Tom, like most men, knew if he sidestepped the question and complimented her, he could stay out of trouble. "Let's get to the show."

Tom locked the door behind him and hurried down two flights of stairs. They went through the outer door, walked a few feet to the old concrete steps, and descended to the sidewalk along Grant Street. As usual, there wasn't a parking spot to be found on either side of the narrow street. "Oh, I forgot to tell you," she said. "There's not going to be the usual Bible study today. The assistant coach is speaking, giving his testimony on why he's a Christian."

That should be entertaining.

"We're having special music by a couple of Brits and refreshments before the game," said Sarah. "And I'll introduce you to the pastor of the local Calvary Chapel church. He arranged it all today."

Tom nodded his head, but he was only half-listening like men sometimes do. His mind was on the game. Maybe this would be the year they beat Penn State. The hostile crowd in the small bowl stadium gave a big hometown advantage. The streets were already bristling with people, and when they got to University Avenue, it became a steady throng. They crossed the old pedestrian bridge with its worn wooden planks next to the stadium. Tom looked down over the side at the Old Mountainlair in the Falling Run hollow. The old building had seen better days. They rounded a corner, walked the length of a football field and crossed the street with a mass of other people heading for the student union, the Mountainlair. They entered, went left down a hallway, and entered a room filled with people. Everyone was talking cheerfully and seemed to be enjoying themselves.

A man not much older than them came up to Sarah. "Sarah," he said. "So good you could come. And this must be Tom. She's said so many great things about you."

They shook hands, and Sarah said, "Tom, this is Pastor Shawn Frazee, and yes, this is my super husband."

Tom sized up the pastor. He was a friendly guy who seemed honestly interested in Tom's well-being. Pastor Shawn spoke, "I'm so glad you made it today. We've got special music, a guest speaker, and refreshments before the game. Drop-in on us tomorrow. Services are at nine and eleven. Sarah knows where the church is on High Street. Hope to see you there. Sorry, I can't talk longer. You know how it is when you're the leader and have to run the show. I'll see you later. And remember the services tomorrow. Bye."

"He's a great guy, Tom," said Sarah. "You'll really like him."

"He left a good first impression."

"Tom, will you get us each a Coke? Things will start soon, and I'll get us some good seats."

"Okay," he said and headed for the refreshment table. He asked the young girl behind the table, "Could I have two Cokes, please?"

"Sure," she said. "Is this your first time here? Can't say I ever saw you at church or one of the studies."

"Yeah, it's my first time, and I'm a little surprised. I was expecting a bunch of goody-two-shoes types, but this seems like any crowd I'd see on campus."

"Bingo. I thought the same thing when I first came, but people here are the same. You got long hairs, no hairs, hippies and straights, married couples and singles, some who wanted to come and some who only came to please someone, and some who just came for the free food." She handed Tom two Cokes. "Here're your drinks. Enjoy."

"Thanks. I'm one who came to please my spouse. Sarah's my wife."

"Sarah?" she asked. "She's a great gal. You're a lucky guy."

"I know. Thanks, again, for the drinks. Bye."

"Okay. Hope to see you and Sarah again soon. Bye."

Tom took the Cokes back to Sarah. "Thanks. I was wondering if you were gonna make it back before it started. Have a seat. The music's about to begin."

The people began to sit down, and two long-haired young men with guitars walked to the front of the room. "Hi," one said with a British accent. "We're glad to be here today. Pastor Shawn asked us to come today. I'm Colm, and this is Allen."

He pointed to the other man who nodded. "We're, as you may have guessed from our accents, a long way from home. We'll be at Pastor Shawn's church tomorrow with special music. We hope you can make it. We're going to do some praise music to our Lord today, and then the Mountaineer's Assistant Coach Bubba Bowdein is going to speak to you for a short while. He got us tickets to a football game, though he tells us, American football is a little different from the football we play back home. So let's get started."

Tom listened as they sang contemporary Christian music. He'd heard of it, but this was his first exposure, and he liked it. It was beautiful. Sarah sang along, and he tried to mouth the unfamiliar words. Some raised their hands as they sang. Tom found this curious but not threatening. It was a lot better than getting shot at on a battlefield in Vietnam.

After ten minutes of singing, they stopped, took their guitars with them, and sat over on the one side. From the back room came a big man. Tom could tell right off that he was a good old boy. He stood in the front of the crowd, smiled, and said with a heavy, deep southern drawl, "For those of you that don't know me, I'm Bubba Bowdein, assistant coach of the Mountaineer Football team. I hope you all come out after this and cheer on your team. They're gonna need it. Them Nittany Lions are tough stuff, but I didn't come here today to talk with you all about football, as important to me as it is.

"As you can tell from the way I talk, I was born and raised down south in the hills of northern Georgia where they do fun things like noodlin', and crawdads ain't only for bait, but supper, too. You'd never know it from lookin' at me now, but I was sick a lot when I was young. One time the doctors weren't sure I'd survive, but I got better and went to UGA, that's the University of Georgia to anyone who don't know, and became a downright good football player, and not the kind our English friends here are used to. I just missed out on being in WWII but lost an older brother in that war.

"I married my high school sweetheart, who's the mother of my three kids. She's also the one who led me to the Lord. I was one wild and crazy young man, and the crowd I hung out with was a crowd that could be rough at times. One night, after some heavy drinkin', I totaled the old car I had. Passed out and run it smack into an oak tree. People said it was a miracle I survived. It was. I got this scar on my head that will always remind me of that night. Why I survived and others who did less than I did, didn't, I don't know, but this I do know. There is a God up above who sent His one and only Son into this ole world to save us from our sins.

"We all are sinners. I think we all know that." He paused for a moment and looked at the gathering. "I met a man last week who said he'd never sinned in his life. Well, I looked him square in the eye and told him I knew he was a sinner. He asked why. I told him he was a liar because he was lyin' about never havin' sinned. Everybody has, and he was lyin' by tellin' me he never had. He got mad at me and stormed off. Listen, truth is still truth even if society don't wanna hear it, cause it ain't politically correct in some people's minds."

"I ain't got much more to say. If you would like to give your life to the Lord, have your sins forgiven, and have Jesus in your heart, I want you to come forward while Colm and Allen sing. Would you do that? Come; give your life to Jesus today."

Colm and Allen got up, went to the front of the room, and stood next to Bubba. They began to sing,

"Got myself some wisdom from a leatherback book
Got myself a Savior when I took a second look
I opened up the pages and what did I find

A black and white portrait of a King who's a Friend of mine

Funny how when you think you're right, everybody else must be wrong

Till someone with fool's wisdom somehow comes along

His voice was strange and the words He said I didn't quite understand

Yet I knew that He was speaking right by the leather-backed book in his hand

Hey, hey, what a day! Fool's Wisdom

Hey, hey, what a day! Fool's Wisdom

Got myself some wisdom from a leather-backed book

Got myself a Savior when I took a second look, Fool's Wisdom."

Tom felt like that ole coach could see right through him. He knew he was a sinner in need of a savior. Any fool would know that, but his feet felt like lead, and he did not move nor did any others.

Bubba spoke, "I know that some of you all here today wanted to come forward and didn't. Don't put it off. Give your life to Him today. You won't regret it."

Bubba raised his hand, lowered his head, and prayed, "May the Lord bless and keep you all, may He shine His ever lovin' grace on you all, and may His face always look upon you all and give you peace. Amen. And one last thang, Go Mountaineers, Whooo!!"

Everyone cheered at this last thing the coach had said, everyone but Tom. He was thinking about what the coach had said. Tom looked at Sarah and said, "I need to talk with the coach."

"Better catch him quick. He has to get to the stadium for the game."

Coach Bubba Bowdein was turning away as Tom caught his big arm. He turned around, looked at Tom, and said, "Boy, you want somethin'? Make it fast. I got to get to the stadium."

Tom said, "Coach, I heard what you said today. So much of what you said hit me right in the bullseye. I thought you'd known me since I was little. Can God forgive anyone, no matter their sin?"

"Yes, He not only can but will when you ask for His free gift of salvation. His Son paid the price with His redeeming blood on a cruel, Roman cross two thousand years ago, and that gift of forgiveness of sins is still available for all."

"Coach, I was a soldier in Vietnam, and I hurt and killed a lot of men. Can He forgive that, too?"

The coach's face was full of compassion, and he spoke, "War's a little bit different ball game. The important thing is you want to be forgiven, right?"

"Yes."

Bubba looked around, saw Pastor Shawn, and called him over to them. "Pastor Shawn," said the coach, "this young man wants to give his life to Christ today. Ain't that so?"

"It is," said Tom. "I have no reservations. I want Him to forgive my sin and make me His."

Tom felt a hand on his arm. It was Sarah. "Oh, Tom. How I've prayed for this moment. I was standing behind you two listening. I'm so happy."

Pastor Shawn put his hand on Tom's and Bubba's shoulders. Sarah completed the four-sided square. Pastor Shawn spoke, "Almighty God, You just heard what this young man said. He wants forgiveness for sins and to be Yours. Forgive him now and fill him with Your Spirit, now and forever. Amen."

The other three echoed, "Amen."

"Welcome to the family of God, Tom," said Pastor Shawn, and he gave Tom a big hug.

"Yeah, welcome Tom," said Bubba. "God loves you, and I'm gonna try to do the same." Tom had never been hugged by a big man like this before, but somehow, it seemed right.

"Tom," Sarah said, "you've made me so happy," and she gave him a big bear hug. She squeezed so hard thatTom thought she was going to break something.

"I feel different," said Tom.

"You are different," said the pastor. "You're a new creation through Jesus Christ, our Lord. Tom, this may seem a little weird to you. It still does when the Lord speaks to me, but He told me, He had His hand on you even before you knew Him, and He has something special for you."

A look of surprise came on Tom's face. "Me? Why would He do that?"

"God has His reasons," said the pastor. "As you learn more, He will reveal more when He wants to let you know. Trust Him."

"I can do that," said Tom.

"And I'll help him," said Sarah.

"Good," added the pastor. "Now, I need to get this place cleaned up, and you two need to get to the football game."

"Okay," Tom and Sarah said together. They looked at each other and smiled.

"Do you need any help?" asked Tom.

"No, thanks. Looks like the others pretty much put everything away while we were praying," said the pastor.

Tom looked around and saw it was so. "Okay," he said. "We'll go to the game, and thanks for all you did for me today."

"Not I," said Pastor Shawn. He pointed to the sky, "Him." He paused. "Get to the game. I'll be in touch."

Tom said, "Thank you, and bye."

As they walked down the hallway arm-in-arm, Sarah spoke, "Things are going to be different, Tom," and she smiled.

They walked out of the building, and Tom looked around. It was like he had never really seen the world before. *Things were going to be different.*

The Mountaineers lost that day even with the capacity hometown crowd cheering them on, but it didn't dampen Tom's spirit a bit. He's been made new. He'd crossed his Rubicon, and there was no turning back.

Epilogue

September 5, 1997, Late Afternoon

"Stop it Joann! I said, 'Stop it!' Cut it out!"

Tom Kenney pushed away from the slobbering kisses. His face was covered. He raised up from his sleeping position and saw his three-legged dog, Tripod, standing four feet away, giving him a big doggy smile. Then, he gave a big and friendly, "Wolf."

"Tripod, it's you!" Tom said in an accusing voice. He looked at the little mutt. His body and tail shook back-and-forth wildly. "Tripod, are you wagging your tail, or is it wagging you?"

Tripod gave an even bigger doggy grin and let out another, "Wolf."

Tom shook his head and looked at his watch. He'd been asleep for a long time. *What crazy dreams. It felt like it was real and I was reliving it again. It seemed so real.*

"Tripod, you'd never believe the crazy dream I had," said Tom. "And I think I'd better not tell Joann I thought your licks were her kisses. Can that be our secret and ours alone?"

"Wolf," Tripod barked and then made a friendly sound, kind of a half gargle, half growl, in his throat.

"I believe that was a yes. I'll make sure you get extra doggy treats when we eventually get home."

Tripod walked a short way down the path that lead home. He turned his head back to look at Tom and let out another, "Wolf."

"Okay, Tripod. I get the drift. Joann sent you to find me, it's supper time, and you're hungry. Okay, give me a moment, and I will be with you."

Somehow, Tripod understood. He turned around toward Tom, yawned, and sat down, never taking his eyes off Tom.

"Okay, I get the picture. You're not leaving till you have me safely home. It will be just a minute." The little dog lay down, still watching Tom, who closed his eyes and began to pray. *Dear Lord, thank You for all You've done for me. I thank You for the Psalms and the stories of Your servant David. When I read about his trials, challenges, successes, and failures recorded in the Bible, I know I'm not the only one who feels like I sometimes do. I'm glad there're stories about David. I'd much rather everyone over the millennia read about the ups and downs of David and not me. I'm glad there's no Book of Tom.*

Just like David, I can say, "I love you, Lord," because You're our fortress, my rock in time of troubles, and deliverer. You are my shield, salvation, and stronghold. You've kept me through the trials. Surely, You've placed people in my life who gave help and comfort. Lord, just like David, You hear my prayers and my cries. No matter how bad conditions are, I can always call out to You because You're there. I don't know what will happen tomorrow, but I know You'll be there when I need You. I can find peace and joy in my relationship with You, the One and only true and living God.

I thank You for Your promise never to leave us. Though I may feel alone, You haven't gone anywhere. You're right here. You said, "I am with you always, even to the end of the age. Never will I leave you, and never will I forsake you." Your promises are true. Lord, help me recognize Your power and plan for my life. I yield my life to You and trust You'll act in Your time and way. Teach me to trust You as much as Job did when he said, "Though You slay me, yet I will trust in You." Thank You for all YI ou have done in my life. Amen.

Tom let out a deep sigh and said, "Okay, Tripod. Let's go. Dog food and treats for you. I hope Jo isn't mad at me for being up here so long. I may be getting the same thing to eat." Tom paused and said, "If she is really mad, I may need a place to stay. Okay if I bunk with you tonight if I need to?"

Tripod looked up at Tom and gave a "wolf" that sounded like a positive affirmation to Tom. "That's great. It's no wonder a dog's man's best friend." The dog stopped and let Tom pet him. Tom wasn't sure who got the most enjoyment from it. "Okay, Tripod. Let's get moving, or she'll be mad at you, too."

The dog let out a little "wolf,"' and they headed down the old, rocky road that led down the mountain to home.

***

On a mountain nearby

"Papa, is he finally asleep?"

"Sí, Mama, he is."

The Hispanic man reached down and took the empty Jack Daniels bottle away. "He's drinking more and more all the time. It's not good for him. It will kill him."

"Sí, Papa. I fear for him. He has all the money and power any man could want, but he is not satisfied. This one thing has escaped him, but you and I both know it will not bring fulfillment. There is an empty place inside him that he cannot fill." She looked at the monitor screen and saw the man praying with a little, three-legged dog next to him. She reached over and turned it off. "His love for the lost gold of Braddock has become an obsession. Even if he gets it, his pleasure in having it will be short, and then he will be wanting again."

"

"Sí, Rosa, but I think it's more than that. He is very good at hiding his desires and feeling, but yes, something long dead in him is stirring. His cold heart is starting to beat again. His frozen heart is slowly thawing."

"I see it, too, Jairo. I worry, and I hope for him." The small, senior woman paused and added, "He needs us."

"You are right, Mama. Years ago, when we left Nicaragua for America, he was a godsend. We needed him."

"And now, he needs us."

"Sí."

The woman placed a blanket over the drunk, sleeping man.

"God sent him when we needed him, and now God has us here at this time because he needs us."

The old man nodded. "Sí, he needs us, more than he can even imagine. He needs us now."

The End

For God has chosen the foolish things of this world to confound the wise; He has chosen the weak things of this world to confound the mighty. 1 Corinthians 1:27

Why *Fool's Wisdom*?

Many people would think the words fool and wisdom do not go together. It's an oxymoron. Usually, the terms don't, but a "fool" can be the wisest of people. A fool or court jester was the only one able to make fun of the king and tell him truths he may not want to hear without fear of being imprisoned or even executed. Some fools have discovered eternal truths the world sees as foolishness. It may be the innocent child whose parents have not converted to "proper" behavior yet, or it may be the person labeled as a fool because those in charge don't want others to see the truths the "fool" does.

Some people the world calls fools because they have an entirely different perspective than what is considered normal. Socrates claimed he was wise because he knew nothing at all. Others like Charlie Chaplin and Harpo Marx became wealthy and famous by being foolish, and Forrest Gump showed even a fool could be successful. The Bible often speaks of fools that are known by their foolish deeds, but it also speaks of the wise fool. Proverbs 1:7 tells us, "The fear of the LORD [is] the beginning of knowledge: [but] fools despise wisdom and instruction," and 1Corintians 3:18 tells us, "Let no one deceive himself. If anyone among you thinks that he is wise in this age, let him become a fool so he may become wise."

I hope you enjoyed *Fool's Wisdom,* and it made you step back and think of what true wisdom and truths really are and where they originate.

Jay Heavner

WANT TO READ MORE?

Braddock's Gold Mystery Series

Braddock's Gold

Hunter's Moon

Fool's Wisdom

Killing Darkness

Florida Murder Mystery Series

Death at Windover

Murder at the Canaveral Diner

Murder at the Indian River

WANT TO HELP THE AUTHOR?

If you enjoyed the book, would you help get the word out? Please tell others about it. Word-of-mouth advertising is the best marketing tool on this planet.

A good review on Amazon, Goodreads, or elsewhere would help with the author being able to keep writing full time. It doesn't have to be long. Thanks.

SIGN UP FOR JAY HEAVNER'S NEWSLETTER

With this, Jay will occasionally keep you informed with new books coming out and anything else special. Feel free to email him at jay@jayheavner.com. His website is www.jayheavner.com. He loves reader feedback.

www.ingramcontent.com/pod-product-compliance
Lightning Source LLC
Chambersburg PA
CBHW020326200626
46814CB00006BB/2433
* 9 7 8 1 7 3 3 6 1 7 4 5 1 *